MW00965718

LOVE TO PUCK

AR

LOVE TO PUCK

The Real Story of an American

Witch

Anne Sharp

Copyright © 2000 by Anne Sharp.

Library of Congress Number: 00-192376
                  Softcover   0-7388-4119-6

All rights reserved. No part of this book may be reproduced or transmitted in any form or by any means, electronic or mechanical, including photocopying, recording, or by any information storage and retrieval system, without permission in writing from the copyright owner.

This is a work of fiction. Names, characters, places and incidents either are the product of the author's imagination or are used fictitiously, and any resemblance to any actual persons, living or dead, events, or locales is entirely coincidental.

This book was printed in the United States of America.

To order additional copies of this book, contact:
Xlibris Corporation
1-888-7-XLIBRIS
www.Xlibris.com
Orders@Xlibris.com

CONTENTS

AR

DEDICATION

For Mama and Amah.

ONE

He was a very religious man, Ken, my boss, though I gather he hadn't always been. He'd been married four or five times, and there had been some tacky scandal surrounding his last job at the state lottery commission, according to the gossips at my office. But supposedly he was all straightened out by the time I met him, a regular family man and a member of God's Family, a Christian group that's very big around here.

God's Family is not a religion in itself. You can belong to almost any Christ-oriented denomination and attend your own regular church and read your own version of the Bible, and God's Family will accept you as long as you agree to live as one of them, by their rules. God's Family has its own prayer meetings and Bible study groups that are more or less mandatory, and also a very strict social organization. Every God's Family person I've ever met lives in the same subdivision as the others—a very nice one, as they tend to recruit among the managing class—and outside of whatever work or other business they need to attend to in the outside world, they associate only with each other.

A woman I used to work with once told me about how she and her husband got involved with them. They were new in town and didn't know anybody, and God's Family just took them in. She said it was very comforting, you had instant friends and they took care of everything for you. If you needed a job, they found one for you. If you needed a blender, they knew who had one to spare and saw that you got it.

One of the reasons God's Family is such a success is it's so cleverly run. It's pretty sizable in terms of members and revenues, but to the people in it it feels small, cozy and safe. The two guys who thought up God's Family—both of whom eventually ended up quitting and turning against it—were smart. They understood that nobody joins a religious group just to feel they belong to that group. They want to feel the group belongs to *them*. God's Family knows how to deliver that illusion.

It really does operate like a family, or most people's idea of a family. When you join you're assigned to a little group within the group, maybe twenty or thirty people, that's managed by an elder. Elders are the ones that tell you what you should be doing, who you should or shouldn't be associating with, how much of your money you should give to God's Family or the various causes it sponsored. I think Ken always had hopes of being an elder, but God's Family were a little too wise for that.

This all happened, Ken and God's Family and everything else, right before the millennium, when Christians were becoming very aggressive. You always heard about Christian groups picketing or boycotting or trying to make something illegal, shooting somebody or blowing something up and saying they were just following God's commands. It was frightening to me, for the simple reason that history tells very clearly what militant Christians do to people like me. With every cross I saw around a neck, with every fish decal I saw on a car, I found myself curling in on myself, feeling less at home in my world, and that's not like me.

The place where I live is kind of strange. Ten miles outside of town are cornfields and citizens' militias and Klan rallies, but here where the university is is one of the most sophisticated towns in Middle America, really an island of astonishing tolerance. The townies tend to be conservative and the university types are more libertarian, but then of course the kids are all radical in either direction, which evens things out.

If you think about it, we all have to be careful here or we'd kill each other. We're just too diverse to be practicably intolerant, and it's always been this way. Even when the university was founded a hundred and fifty years ago it was very progressive. It was the first public university to let in women and nonwhites. There was even a time when the homeopathic medical college almost beat out the traditional medical school for funding and enrollment. (It got phased out about sixty years ago, though I wouldn't be surprised if they brought it back now, with the alternative medicine boom; it would be a big moneymaker.) The university has always profited from its openness. A lot of Jewish academics from the East who couldn't get past the anti-Semitism in the Ivy League schools came here in the early twentieth century, and now, because of all the wars and repression and genocides all over the world, we have great Eastern

European and Asian and African and Arabian scholars doing their work and making their homes here. The local Klan isn't thrilled but there's not a lot they can do.

They tried to stage a rally last summer—nine lumpy men in nightmare ghost costumes, walking around on the roof of the police station, the only place the city council could think of where they wouldn't be mashed to death by all the counter-protesters; about five hundred showed up, and were they mad! They just screamed their lungs bloody. I doubt anyone even heard what those pointy-hooded twerps up on the roof were moaning through their bullhorns. The Klan certainly didn't get their message across, and looked pretty unglamorous, so I doubt they made any recruits that day. I don't know why they even showed up, except just for the joy of browning off all those people. That might have been enough for them. It seems sometimes the only pleasure angry people have is making other people angry.

Ken loved demonstrations. He was very active in the Christian protest movement. In fact that was his real passion; for sure he wasn't very interested in being our boss. In the context of what he was supposed to be doing at work, and how important that was supposed to be, it was amazing what he got away with. It was his philosophy that being our managing director was not necessarily a full-time job. Not over forty hours; hardly even thirty actually. Twenty or twenty-five was more like it. "As long as my work gets done, who cares?" he said.

And it did get done. Ken was a great delegator and a terrific threatener. So he had plenty of time on company time to do his real work, which, he was always telling people, was the work of God.

When he first hired me, he was very deep into his involvement with SOS, an activist group which wasn't officially affiliated with God's Family but did have a lot of its people in it. SOS was one of those groups, like those Klan marchers on the police station roof, that seemed less interested in winning sympathy for its cause than in beating people into a frenzy while making sure there were as many television cameras around as possible.

Whether SOS had any hopes of literally accomplishing what it said it was out to do, I seriously doubt. Nobody even seemed to know what

SOS stood for. I've heard them say it meant Save Our Sons or Save Our Schools, Stop Organized Sodomy, even Stamp Out Sodomites. Who knows anything but what they actually did?

The thing that put everybody over the edge happened that fall, about a year after I started at SMAT. It was just after Labor Day and the public schools were opening again for the first day of the new school year. Our school district, which was known as a change leader in experimental education, had just gone through a very controversial process of deciding to open a new high school just for homosexual students, both boys and girls. These kids, there were six of them, had been tormented and even physically attacked by other kids. The school board had ruled that these kids deserved a public education without being put in danger because of other people's prejudices, and if giving them separate classes in a separate building was what it took, they'd just do it.

SOS had been following this all along, and was raising a very big stink about it. Although it was supposed to be a secret, they found out where the gay kids' classes would be held—probably from some God's Family person who worked in the school board office—and on opening day were camped out on the steps of the building, about fifty of them, all rehearsed with chants and songs and tricked out with all sorts of T-shirts and signs like "God Loves Homosexuals, God Hates Homosexuality" and "Stop Teaching Our Kids to Be Perverts." The reporters and television news cameras were all there, too; they loved an SOS bash.

The police had to come and escort the kids to their classes. They forced open a feeble little crack in the packed crowd of SOS demonstrators so the kids could push their way up the stairs. In order to move, these poor kids had to actually press their bodies up against these people who were screaming "Go in there and you're damned to hell!" and shoving "Sin Kills" signs under their noses. The kids were brave and pretty smart; I'd read interviews with a couple of them, and they were as prepared as they could have been for this. They said nothing and just looked over all the shrieking heads towards the doors they hoped could be dragged open, somehow, so they could get inside.

Then something happened. Apparently the thicket of SOS people blocked the view of the cameras, because I never saw pictures on TV or in the papers, but according to the boy it happened to, Ken knocked the books he was holding out of his arms. Ken said the kid hit him with the books, but there wasn't a mark on Ken—it was the kid who fell and hit the concrete steps with his jaw. Not one of those SOS people who'd been packing their bodies against him so he could barely move a moment before were there to catch him when he fell and cracked his face open on that step.

The kid said Ken shoved and kicked him and yelled something at him I won't dirty your mind with here, and some of the kids and a reporter from the *Press-Dispatch* testified that this really happened, but Ken denied it. The SOS people said the kid just tripped and fell. Still, the cops arrested Ken and photographed and fingerprinted him and put him in a cell, and then he had to go to court, where they set him a bail, something like $500.

But Ken wouldn't pay it. He wouldn't let his wife pay it either. The other SOS people who ended up in jail with him (the protest had gone on all day, with people trying to get into the building and disrupt classes and throw things through the windows) had decided to continue their civil disobedience by refusing to pay bail, saying that paying would be admitting that the state had a right to arrest them when actually they weren't doing anything illegal, according to God's law.

It was a big mess. There wasn't room for all the SOS people in the jail downtown so they had to put them in one of the city garages, all hot and full of noxious fumes. But Ken and his friends stuck it out. I think they also tried to get up a hunger strike too, but it didn't go over as well as the bail strike.

Apart from what happened on the schoolhouse steps, it was a scandal in itself how much it was costing the city to keep these people in their garage, as the strike stretched out from days into weeks. And there was a third source of misery, what the whole SOS affair was doing to SMAT, the place I worked for, that Ken was supposed to be running.

Ken had managed to get in the papers and on television by turning his face towards every camera and shooting his mouth off to everyone with a microphone. And though it's true he never mentioned where he worked, it was a matter of public record, right in his police file, that he was managing director of SMAT. I could see exactly what was coming.

13

The very last thing in this space-time continuum that SMAT is supposed to be is involved in an anti-homosexual crusade. First of all, it's a nonprofit organization, and there are laws about not getting involved in politics if you want to keep your tax-exempt status. Not to mention that in any human population a certain percentage will be homosexually oriented, even the gearheads who belong to SMAT; you have to remember things like that if you want to keep up your membership.

But if there's one thing I've learned from everything I've been through, it's that once a person's reached a certain level of power as an authority figure, a magic is conferred on him. No matter how cruel or stupid he is, no matter how much damage and devastation he creates, no matter how much people hate him and secretly badmouth him, no one will challenge him to his face. He starts believing himself that he has an infallible right to do whatever he wants; he declares himself a god, and the others bend down and from then on will be on their knees to that person. Call it the Caligula effect. The only thing that can stop it is an assassin.

Managing director is the highest-level (and highest-paid) post in SMAT and its stand-in for God. He's supposed to set an example for all his employees, inspire confidence in SMAT's members and fellows (enough, at least, to fork over the astonishing dues asked of them), the people who buy its publications and attend its seminars and conferences, its board of trustees, and the scholarly and professional community that it's supposed to be promoting. It's a nonaffiliated organization; all it really has keeping its butt off the pavement are donations and subscriptions, and the only thing it has to recommend itself is its reputation. If it were no longer prestigious to be a member or fellow of the society, or to attend its conventions or publish papers in the *SMAT Journal*, it would evaporate.

And there was Ken in a puddle of oil in the city garage, telling the board president that he had higher personal priorities than going back to work in time to attend the monthly board meeting.

We weren't supposed to say anything to anybody about all this. Any calls that came into SMAT complaining about Ken or asking questions were supposed to be referred to the board president and Santa, our operations administrator. But Santa and the board president didn't have to actually answer the phone, so they never heard the worst of it. Being in charge of pee-arrh, I had it all coming to me.

Because Ken had gotten on the national news, I was getting calls from everywhere you could think of, and they were furious. I had members threatening to cancel their memberships, putting stop payments on donation checks. (That was around the time when our financial situation started its serious slide.) We had an author withdraw a paper we were set to publish, one of the few really good ones we'd gotten that year.

The board finally pulled itself together with a tremendous effort and with all its might put out a teensy one-paragraph press release, timidly murmuring that Ken's views might not necessarily be exactly those endorsed by SMAT. What integrity, what character. *They* had hired Ken for the job (mostly because he was the cheapest candidate); *they* knew what he was, and it was up to *them* to control him. They should have fired him right then, and they had perfect grounds for it. It was right in his contract that absent an "act of God," he had to attend every board meeting as a condition of employment.

But the board chose to ignore this. He was their boy, and their choice was either to support him whatever he did and insist he was wonderful, or admit they'd made a mistake. Well, you knew what they'd do. Open any management theory book and it will tell you a successful administrator never admits a mistake. Who doesn't want to be successful?

"They wouldn't be making a fuss like this if he'd been in jail for something 'politically correct', like animal rights," one of the trustees said right in front of me. She even tried to get the board and staff to take up a collection and pay the bail ourselves, but someone must have pointed out that paying Ken's bail wouldn't necessarily mean he'd come back to work; he might go right back to the school and start busting kids' heads again.

Working at SMAT that fall was even more unpleasant than usual. People's feelings broke out in a way they hadn't before. This is a corollary of the Caligula effect. When a person dares to set himself above ordinary workers and pretend that he has special wisdoms, special skills and intuitions, and when other people anoint that person and say yes,

AR

you are better and smarter than us, those anointers from then on have a stake in believing it really is so. Despite the evidence of their own senses, whatever disasters follow, the underlings will go on clinging to the desperate creed that what this person says is right and he knows what he's doing. But when Ken sat in that rotten garage and told the reporters that despite his being its official leader and public representative, SMAT came absolutely last as far as he was concerned, everything cracked. All that had been held together by that delusionary trust we had put in him fell in pieces.

We all suffered, except Santa. Being officially in charge of SMAT with Ken gone, and with no one else with any authority paying attention, she went on a regular massacre. The first thing she did was fire a friend of mine who Santa's predecessor had hired. She was the last holdout from the old regime, and Santa preferred her own people; they gave her less resistance. It was terrifying. She did it with her office door open, so everybody could hear.

Three people quit, including the first competent marketing person we'd ever had. The desktop publishing system went down, and our computer coordinator (one of Ken's God's Family friends) couldn't figure out why, so the October issue of the *SMAT Journal* had to come out on Thanksgiving. Three federal grant applications that we'd worked on for a month just went for nothing because Ken was supposed to authorize them and hadn't; we found them on his credenza three days after the filing deadline.

One woman went into the hospital with asthma; someone else had a miscarriage. We were edgy and exhausted and wondered why we were even coming to work. Who cared? (except Santa, who scanned the electronic key-card system every day to make sure we were all there on time.)

We realized we'd been tricked, thinking what we did mattered. Now our slightest misgivings were confirmed. Ken didn't just act like a maniac; he was a maniac. The trustees really were shifty incompetents. Our members really were pathetic victims of a confidence scheme designed to screw them into turning their money and time and scholarly work over to a chaos factory posing as a reputable professional society. And we, the little worklings whose labors made it all possible, weren't even in on the take. Our salaries, which would be below industry standards if there were such things, weren't even worth the souls we'd sold in order to earn them.

Ken eventually agreed to leave jail and behave himself. His God's Family elder told him he would better serve Christ by going back to his job and supporting his wife and children than by staying in the SOS bail strike. He wasn't happy but he came back to us and put in his four or five hours a day, mostly in his office with the lights dimmed and the door closed.

When Ken was in jail, one of my friends at work asked me if I'd write a letter we could all send to the newspaper, with our names signed to it, telling everyone that we didn't agree with what Ken had done. The board came out with its press release right after that, so we never did send the letter. But I think I should have done it anyway, even though I would have been fired for it—so what? Considering all the difference all my loyalty and good works for the greater glory of SMAT made for my eventual job security, why did I even go to work that day of the demonstration? Why wasn't I at that school instead, putting myself between Ken and that kid?

One day, early on in the whole bail strike affair, I just couldn't work anymore, couldn't concentrate, and gave up and went home early—I figured Santa would get me if she wanted to, whether I gave her cause or not. I couldn't eat dinner that night. I fed and watered the plants and cats, got into bed and pulled the covers up and thought, I'm never coming out again. I didn't want to be part of a world where people took up collections for people who smashed little boys' faces, where people worshiped a God who had so little respect for human life.

Then Padraic came over. He had a present for me, wrapped in a piece of purple velvet. It was a beautiful thing, a knife with a diamond-shaped blade, carbon steel, with an inlaid handle of obsidian and mother of pearl. I asked what was it for, to kill Ken with.

"This is your athame," Padraic said, closing my hand around the handle.

Blessed Be!

HAR

If Padraic and I had been husband and wife or boyfriend and girlfriend, we would never have done what we did together. It was because we'd known each other just as casual friends, liked each other but weren't at all involved in any sense, that we could take up such an intimate thing between the two of us. And it was necessary that we not really consider each other that much; it had to be an almost impersonal undertaking, so we could encourage each other easily or point out things we'd over-looked without giving offense. And not knowing each others' faults, we could trust each other better.

We were nervous just starting out, and who could blame us. When we went out to buy the candles and the cloth and wine, we went together. So we wouldn't feel so weird. The truth was that in those first days we had no real confidence about what we were doing. We had some books, things we'd found at bookstores or sent away for: *Drawing Down the Moon, The Spiral Dance, Lady Sheba's Book of Shadows.* (We'd learned not even to bother looking for "occult" books at the library; these are the first ones that get stolen and the last to get replaced.) There were some magazines and a newsletter I'd started subscribing to, and we'd also found some online things which were mostly worthless. And then we had our own ideas and beliefs, and that was it. We didn't know anyone else remotely involved in this sort of thing. As time went on and we got more courage we got in touch with some local practitioners, including a woman we'd seen on television who turned out to be helpful. But at this point we weren't convinced they knew what they were doing any more than we did. They say there are some who have practiced these traditions for generations, passed them down through their families, but how can you tell when people are telling the truth about these things? It's not like they have a pedigree to show you to prove it. And who says they're any more real than we are, that they hold the license to do this and we don't?

Padraic and I didn't know anything, and we knew it. We just had plenty of nerve to do what we did, without authoritative guidance or sanction. And essentially we were on the right track, though we got so much wrong at first. We thought you could just make up your own rules and it would work anyway because the intention was clear, like a do-it-yourself wedding. Which is true to some extent. But as with cooking or music or anything, you had really better know the rules before you start improvising.

The one thing we did then that we were later really proud of—and grateful for, considering what came later—was that before starting in with anything, we made some basic decisions about *why*, and how we were going to go about this. Long before we ever went shopping for knives and herbs and chalices, we made some rules. Everything we would do was to be positive. Nothing we did should intentionally harm a living thing. Nothing was to be done for profit, or to gain power over others. Everything we did would be private, but nothing was to be secret. We would reject publicity, but share all the knowledge we could if it meant helping anyone.

A lot of people, including Wiccans, when I tell them this ask me, "Why wouldn't you want power?" I can never make them understand, power was the *last* thing we wanted. If you want power, be a politician or business administrator, or better yet, have a child. Then throw your power around—see if it makes you or anyone else happy.

People are in love with the idea of magic. If you are weak and aimless, you can make yourself feel masterful doing tricks with chants and blood and flames. If you are a boss and feel guilty about what you're doing to the people under you, you can tantalize your conscience by thinking about the people you've squashed giving you the evil eye. Revenge is a dish most easily digested with an empty mind. But we wanted *wisdom*. We wanted to *learn*.

And we had studied Wicca and all its attendant lore and mythology for a long time before we even dared to try the rites. We did experiment a bit with magic before our first official esbat, but it seemed so innocuous, just a preliminary exercise. There was a recipe Padraic found in some little paperback he found at Art's Books, supposedly an ancient Italian recipe for love cakes. The writer gave an updated recipe, saying it should work just as well. Basically all you did was make up a batch of Jiffy mix and add some ground-up Italian sausage and semisweet morsels. You baked it in muffin pans and served the little cakes to anyone who was making your life unhappy by fighting. It calmed them down and made them affectionate and easy to manage.

I hadn't been at SMAT long when Padraic showed me this recipe, but I was already tired of the way people at work were acting, and I knew they would eat just about any kind of cake or doughnut, no matter how disgusting it was. I actually tried baking a batch of the love cakes one night, but after we tasted one I threw out the rest and gave up. The cakes were edible, but strange. Padraic thought they might have come out better if he had helped bake them, as working the spell together would have increased the cone of power. But it seemed to me that it was the recipe itself that had let me down.

I had heard that the secret of spells is that they are an oral tradition which must be passed on person to person, to protect their magic from outsiders who would steal or abuse it. That's why whenever spells are written down, one of the key ingredients or some important step is left out. I suppose this is one of the reasons people who are Wiccan by family tradition have an edge on us converts.

But then, every Wiccan knows that printed words are magic in themselves, for the reason that people will believe in and be swayed by just about anything they see written on a page. When I think of the serious consideration Padraic and I gave even the old drugstore paperbacks we collected, I'm amazed, both by our faith and by the fact that we didn't come to any serious harm monkeying around with them.

One of the things that we did get right at the beginning was that certain things about Wicca are simply common sense: that the full moon is the most powerful time of month, midnight is the most powerful time of the sun cycle, and thirteen is the right number for a coven. But we weren't about to wait for eleven new recruits before we got started, and I'm glad we didn't, because together we made the perfect beginning.

I had made cloaks for us to wear for this occasion, and we liked them so much we stuck with them from then on. Some people thought they were costumey—and they are; so, I might add, are the Pope's. But they are practical. They're warm, and if you're standing in wet grass or snow in the middle of the night, you need that comfort if you're going to concentrate. It's a cool warmth my cloaks give, with the soft fine wool on the outside blocking the wind and the satin on top of the head and along the sides of the face and the arms and back holding the warmth to you, but letting the freshness of the air communicate itself to your skin. You can wear whatever you want underneath; I've worn it in winter with nothing else but boots and felt no cold whatsoever. The thing is, my cloaks don't restrict you the way a coat does. And with your eyes shaded by your hood, if you have it up, and your hands able to draw up into your nice big sleeves when you aren't using them, you feel secret and private and close to yourself, which seems to intensify your power. It also slows down your movements, making the feeling of reverence stronger.

Clothing was something of an issue when the Gulo Coven first got started. A lot of things we'd read strongly recommended that the rites be done skyclad, which means nude. It's supposed to make whatever magick you produce stronger. That's plausible enough—just think of all the times that nudity has aroused a particularly powerful emotion in *you*—but it seems to me to presuppose a climate where it never gets below seventy degrees and there's no mosquitos or picker bushes to interfere with your concentration. Which would indicate to me that skycladness is not an ancient Wiccan tradition, but something that was invented in California. Certainly in most places in Europe where the Old Religion is practiced, there are few times of the day or year when you can be comfortably naked outdoors. And where I live, there are also children out past curfew and voyeurs and patrol cars. Still, there is something powerful about baring yourself to the sky. Even if you don't literally reveal your skin, to open your rites to the elements around you is the best way to go about getting in touch with the earth spirits. Padraic and I have always believed this, and whenever possible this is something we've put into practice.

Neither Padraic nor I lived in a place with its own private yard, and neither felt comfortable out in the woods by ourselves at night. We decided to try out our rites in what seemed like the coziest compromise between wildness and cultivation, a little clearing in an area by the municipal golf course next to my apartment complex. It wasn't completely isolated. Even at midnight, people drove down the dirt road by the course maybe five or six times an hour. But they couldn't see through the trees, and if we were quiet and cautious there was no reason why anyone should

AR

ever know we were there. Even if we were caught, the worst thing they could do was make us go home, we reasoned.

The very first ceremony we ever created together was very short, and not very strong because it was almost totally invented by us; we were still learning, still full of that mad sense of beginner's luck. But it was by far the most beautiful rite that either of us would play a part in for a long time.

It was a cool clear night and there was a full pale spring moon. When we got to the clearing, we set out two tray tables in the grass—just sopped with dew, so it looked like silver in the moonlight—and laid out the things we'd use. Napkins, incense, a little brass gong, glasses, a thermos, a mortar and pestle, a fondue pot and a sterno can (we were so unpretentious then!), little bags of the vegetable and animal matter we needed, a lighter, and three candles. Padraic lit the first candle, a white one.

"In the beginning was life."

We passed our hands over it, to feel its warmth. Now a red one, which I lit from the first one.

"Out of life came love. And out of love came life."

The black one we lit simultaneously, at both red and white, by tipping their wicks all together at once. He held the white, I held the red. We held the black together.

"And after life and love comes change, renewal. The three principles of life together, a cycle. Each lighting the way to continuity, continual birth and rebirth, a cycle. Life, love, change. Life, love, change. Life. Love. Change. Life."

We passed the candles between us, three times, in a circle. In turn we would blow them out, then light them on the next candle to be passed from hand to hand. Then when the candles had all lighted each other, they went into their holders. We held the sweet incense in the flame of life till it started a good smoulder, and then held hands standing over the candles, making an enclosing circle with our arms. Then we gave each other sips of the special warm spiced wine Padraic had prepared, and ate the little cakes I'd baked. This was our first love feast.

It sounds sexual, the ritual performed by a man and a woman together alone at night, and it was but not in the carnal sense that might suggest.

There was a symbolic power to it that we liked and often tried to recreate in our rites afterwards. To have the two forces in humanity most at odds with each other, man and woman, come together for such a pure, disinterested purpose is a joy to nearly everyone who experiences it. But eroticism never entered our coven, not at this point, certainly not between Padraic and me.

We were always careful not to talk too much about what we did, especially around people who wouldn't understand. But as discreet as we were, once we had started, we found that we couldn't keep it just to ourselves. Power attracts. And the power that even two people can generate, working together in perfect agreement to a single purpose, is so unusual in North American culture, especially in such a reserved and competitive urban village like the one we live in, that it just draws in those who are longing for harmony.

Fortunately, the people who tended to pick up on our synergistic power were for the most part people we were happy to share our experiences with. The Monday after our first esbat I ran into Dana, who I liked but hardly ever got a chance to talk to, in the break room at work. Somehow we got onto the subject. Dana said, "I always wanted to try it but I was always afraid it would be too sick and witchy. I want to be good, like a good Witch."

I took a chance and told her about what Padraic and I had done. Dana was so excited that neither of us got anything done the whole rest of the day. She insisted that Padraic and I let her come along next time we did our rites. Then Padraic got a call from a friend of his who said he'd just had a feeling that Padraic had something very important to tell him.

Two men, two women, drawn together by something none of us understood, that was becoming increasingly precious to us. This must be something wonderful. I started to study more, to try to learn about this thing before I got deeper into it. But even at this stage my doubts were beginning to be calmed by an understanding that this was good. I knew more or less what I was doing by then, and it was all right to lead the others, cautiously, along the path Padraic and I were making.

The next time we came together there were five of us. There was me

23

and Dana, and Padraic and his friend Chris, and Chris' friend Nils. Nils seemed a little shy, maybe because he was so much younger than us. I know I felt very middle aged around him. He had a little baby seal face and cropped hair with bangs, the way students were wearing it then, the way we used to wear it when I was his age. He looked about seventeen, and I kept thinking, I could be this boy's mother. I tried not to be condescending, to put him at ease. It must have worked, because he stayed with us much longer than I would have expected.

The more people we had with us at our esbats, the better it was, because we learned more; individuals shared readings and did research that they could then bring back to the group. We started going back to our original contacts, and now that we were part of the same clan so to speak, they started to make more sense to us. Also, I think they trusted us more, since we'd proved ourselves not to be amateurs or sickos, but real devotees of the craft.

Some of the most helpful advice we had at that time came from the woman we'd contacted when we were just starting out, who called herself Djanga Beldam. She was more or less the unofficial spokeswoman for the Wiccan community in our area, such as it was; the television and newspaper people always interviewed her on Halloween or when they wanted to do a story on love potions. She lived by herself in a little cottage near Maple Lake. At the time I met her she wasn't a member of a coven; she practiced as a lone Witch, or what we call a solitary. She was extremely encouraging when we first went to meet her, when we were just starting out. She listened to what we had been doing, and said that essentially we seemed to be doing everything right. She gave us a copy of Shakti Gawain's *Creative Visualization*, which she said would help us clarify our goals. That was a great feeling, to have that kind of acceptance from a real Witch.

When the Gulo Coven was first forming itself, I had thought that meeting once a moon was enough, that more would be too much of a demand on people's time. But none of them could ever keep track of what phase the moon was in, and as it happened they actually preferred meeting once a week, so that's what we did. That turned out to be crucial to our development as a coven. So was the weather. Usually, in our climate, there is no spring; winter just drizzles on more and more drearily until June, when the switch flips and it's suddenly a 90-degree steambath. But that year we had the first real, Easter-basket spring I can ever remember, warm and green and fragrant, followed by an extraordinarily long summer that started in May and gave us radiant days and cozy frostless nights well into October. So we got in a lot of time together, under the most wonderful conditions. The winter months would slow us down somewhat; when you're up against blizzards and freezing rain and the flu, you can't anticipate regular togetherness. But by that fall we had eight or nine regulars, and so many visitors that once or twice we even made thirteen. I came to love our Friday night meetings. Sometimes our celebrations would last two or three hours, and then we'd all go out for a snack at the Cadillac Diner or the all-night doughnut shop (of course, we'd leave our cloaks in our cars).

When Padraic gave me that beautiful athame, it was a spiritual milestone for me. Up until then I had been using an old carbon steel paring knife, something that could be inconspicuously retired to the kitchen in case Wicca didn't decide to accept me. Because that's how I thought of it then; it was letting me play with it, flirt with it, but did I have a right to it? would I pass the test?

I must have. Because that same week of the athame the coven voted to make me their High Priestess. Up until then we had been sharing sacramental duties, a different one of us officiating each time on a rotating basis. But it was a lot of trouble, all the planning and keeping track of whose turn it was to lead, who was going to buy the candles next, etc. Nils suggested it would just be easier if we put one person in charge of the rituals, and since I had always been the coven den mother anyway I should do it permanently. Padraic seconded this, and then the vote made it official.

It was the biggest honor I'd ever been given, and I took it very seriously, what it meant. I thought of the Hierophant (I'm not really a cartomancer, but I do use the Tarot occasionally in meditation) and considered that if you become preoccupied with the formal structure of religion you tend to lose its essence. Religion is just the house, spirituality is what lives in it. My priestesship wasn't going to be about bossing people and making rules. I would listen to my covenmates, interpret their needs into living symbols that would fortify their lives.

And that wasn't always so easy, because none of us had quite the same needs or ideas about what we were up to. We were still learning, reading, dreaming, having inspirations (as we would always continue to do, as any coven should do), contributing our revelations to the group, and not everybody liked what each of us brought to it. I saw the first signs of real trouble when Nils started talking about Aleister Crowley and the Golden Dawn.

"He really was great," Nils said. "He was a real magician. The major Witch of the twentieth century. Like we could be for the twenty-first."

"He was a Satanist," Padraic said.

"No he wasn't. He was like us. He was brilliant! You should read him."

"Yeah," Padraic said, "I bought *Magick in Theory and Practice* once, I got about to the third page and gave up. Totally incoherent. He was on drugs."

"Wrong, you're so wrong."

"What do you mean, he was a heroin addict. I'm supposed to take spiritual guidance from a guy who couldn't even get off heroin? *Mick Jagger* got off heroin!"

"Read *White Stains*," Nils said.

"Yeah, you know so much. You can't even say his name. It's CROW-lee, not CROWL-ee."

It was a wonder that Nils kept showing up at esbats, Padraic was so mean to him. And Chris, who I'd assumed was his special friend, never defended him; he seemed to think it was funny and appropriate, how Padraic kept teasing poor Nils about Crowley. "Think of a *Golden Dawn*," he said to me once, with Nils right there. "Who would want a *Golden Dawn*? A dawn made out of metal? A cold, hard, greedy dawn?"

This was not at all in the spirit of what our practices were supposed to be about. I finally told Padraic to cut it out, and tried to make it up to Nils, being extra nice and taking him aside to give him special lessons in the craft. He seemed so young and vulnerable, in need of protection. How anyone could think otherwise, I couldn't understand.

Now that we had a High Priestess officiating, our rites went much more smoothly. The do-it-yourself, everybody-pitch-in approach was fun at first, but ultimately we gave it up for the same reasons I gave up on the Unitarians and went over to Wicca.

Our Unitarian church here in town is very much dedicated to incorporating diversity and inclusivity into its liturgy, which is all to its credit, but it got to the point that when you went to a service, there was no sense of spirituality at all, or even sharing with a group, just this weird tension: what's going to happen *now*? Anything could happen; it was like open mike night at a folk bar. Somebody would get up and do a reading of a Native American author, and then somebody'd play the piano, then someone would stand up and stop everything dead by making a spontaneous speech, and you'd be looking at your program, okay, next we all sing the chant to Gaia with the hand movements: how do they go again? If you're constantly concentrating on just keeping the ceremony going, rather than on why you're actually doing it, it's like a bunch of actors without a director, eternally workshopping a play that'll never be performed. It frustrates you and wears you out. At some point, you have to just work out your blocking, learn your lines and go out there and *do* it. And *then*, the beautiful and real and satisfying things can happen.

I believe also that you need a sense of predictable form in a religious service for safety's sake. Religion is like sex; people bring their deepest emotions to it, especially in Wicca, and their reactions to various stimuli you offer them, the words, the music, the waft of the incense or even just the lateness of the hour, can be strong and unpredictable. You and they both need to know that you're safe together, that there are methods in place to guide each other through whatever gets stirred up so that everything remains in control and has a positive outcome.

Some Wiccans regularly use dance in their rituals as a way of dealing with this sort of emotional energy. It can also be used for inducing altered or heightened states of consciousness just in itself; movement can be a powerful magick! Some people were disappointed in those early days that the Gulo Coven didn't do more dancing, just as they regretted the absence of nudity and sex. But the fact is that most of us come from a culture where most of the time people just don't feel like dancing. The most dancing most members of the Gulo Coven ever did in their lives was at a contra dance at the Grange Hall, or at parties or clubs when they were drunk enough not to feel embarrassed and inhibited. It's my philosophy as a priestess that you don't want to be in a position of "getting" people to do something during the rites, so though I do try to introduce dancing now and then when the group dynamics seem propitious, I don't push it. Very rarely, in rare moods, a spontaneous dance will break out, and these are definitely the best. The one dance we've used with most regularity over the years is one that was introduced to us one night by a visitor, and it's not a traditional circle dance or a join-hands thing. Everyone just does the dance, separate, star-scattered, the way we've danced all our lives in darkened halls to pounding pop music. Only this time the darkness is the night itself, and maybe a drummer drums or a piper pipes, but the music is ourselves, singing the chorus, "I just wanna celebrate!" And why not? What better way to end a Wiccan gathering than with a song by Rare Earth?

The spot that the Gulo Coven had chosen as its meeting place was under some trees by a brook at the edge of the golf course, not far from the spot of our very first esbat, just three minutes' walk from my building. It was perfect because you had the open sky, and the nonhuman living things around you, the trees, the grass and plants, the rabbits and birds, and the little stream with its inhabitants. There were flocks of ducks and very aggressive geese that lived there in the warm months that would yell at you if you got too close to them; we ceded them their territory, and they in turn considerately avoided soiling our magic circle.

We loved to hold our rites in this serene place, tamed by humans, inhabited by nature. The water and the chimes, the aroma of wax and tickle of grasses against your toes, gave you back things that you thought had been taken from you forever. I would usually go home after our meetings and have a wonderful deep sleep, then sing to myself the rest of the weekend, until Sunday night, when the dread set in. I'd remember I had to go back, and then the sick headaches would start. I wouldn't be able to sleep, which would put me in the worst possible condition for facing the staff meeting on Monday.

It had been plain to me from my very first interview with Ken that he was insane, and nothing I saw of him after that did anything to contradict that first impression. I had come to the interview in my navy blue power suit, ready with all the fake answers they expect you to give about what accomplishment in your last job you were most proud of, and what you think your worst weakness is (that weakness of course actually being a strength), and what you expect to be doing in ten years (be in *this* job, of course), when suddenly Ken started grabbing at a map tacked by the side of his desk with colored pins stuck all over it.

"Look, look at all this area we don't have coverage for," he gabbled, putting his hands all over it. I had no idea what he was talking about. He rattled on for minutes about things I couldn't possibly be expected to understand, and it was all I could do to just keep my eyes focused, when he suddenly asked me, "You have trouble relating to people? You seem . . . diffident."

I think he had already decided on me. They can smell it on you, when you're miserable and tired, when you're ready to give in and take what they've got for you. And when Santa called and asked if I wanted the job, though my stomach ached for days after I accepted it I knew I had no choice. I had debts to repay, I had cats to support, and I had to eat too; I had to pay my rent and reimburse my landlord for that hole in the wall where my sewing machine had gone through it. And didn't I want some-day to be able to get that poor old machine fixed? There was no ques-tion; the market was dry, there were simply no other jobs. I had to be a good grown-up, sell my time and energy to this SMAT place, and never let them know how I hated it. And I did it. Through all the time I worked under Ken, I was always totally supportive of him, did everything he said, smiled and never gave him a hint of backtalk. I think if you ever asked him, he'd say, "Oh, yeah, Margaret really likes me, she's a great little gal." Being liked was always the difference between life and death at SMAT.

Which is why nothing ever happened to me while he was there. I just stood watching other people coming out of his office in tears.

He was a crazy man, but crafty too. Maybe his babbling, distracted act was meant to keep you confused so he could slip whatever he was smuggling past you, or slip it to you without you knowing it. He'd call staff meetings and spend half the hour just rambling over whatever came into his mind, esoteric stuff about fiscal years and micromanagement you couldn't have followed if you'd wanted to, and when you'd try to say something he'd cut you off. He didn't want to hear you; he only wanted a reaction. He loved to tease you, and get other people to join in. He would call your extension and holler at you over the speakerphone. He would mark up the final draft of your report because you'd written "the 1970s" instead of "the 1970's," and go crosseyed when you tried to tell him why that wasn't quite right. He went to a seminar once that said employees in a service industry (and SMAT, I suppose, was a service industry) should answer their phones by the third ring, so he'd call everybody to make sure they did it. You'd better run away from whoever you were talking with, abandon your computer without saving your work, put all your calls in progress on hold, to make that third ring, or it was into Ken's office with you to face that veiny face and pummeling torrent of put-downs.

The trustees loved Ken. Ken would go into their meetings and be so charming, tell them what a great job he was doing, that they would purr with delight. No one ever contradicted these glowing reports Ken gave of himself; how would they ever get a chance? The only time the trustees ever entered the building was on the day of their meeting, when they'd swagger in, grab their coffee and snacks, go into the meeting room, close the door and roar with laughter for an hour and a half, then come out and stare at us on their way out. All they knew of us was what Ken told them in that room, and of course what we wrote in our monthly reports, which was what Ken had told us to say. There is no more powerful spell than the written word.

The power relationship makes us hypocrites. People I worked with would sit around and mutter mutiny behind Ken's back, then smile and nod and make fake laughs when he turned his attention to them, as though he had the power to chop their heads off. Of course, he did, which made it all the more tense. We had no union, we had no contracts. SMAT knew we had no other job prospects; otherwise, why would we be there?

There is a thing that happens in a workplace when everyone knows that anyone can be gotten rid of at any time. The wolfish part of every individual comes out, and each one looks at the others and thinks, yumm, who's the weakest one here? It becomes fun to go after the ones that have bothered you, that you think aren't as good as you, that don't belong. Once they're marked, through an obvious social slight, a snide comment made in public, a whispering campaign, the others either join in or stay out of the way so they don't get nipped when the biting starts. And once they've started in on you, it's best if you can get out, because they'll keep at you till you're ripped beyond recognition. What's saddest is that the ones they choose for their meals are often the ones with no chance of starting over someplace else. Too old or nervous, or not too sharp. And even if they're not, even if they're actually the brightest, most conscientious workers in the whole place, that's no protection. There are ways of making anybody look bad; who can truly do their best when they're surrounded by people who hate them and want them to fail?

I would hear crying in the bathroom stalls. I saw people go to the hospital with bleeding ulcers and asthma attacks. I saw nervous collapses and alcoholic breakdowns and divorces. And in the middle of this carnival of agony I'd see my coworkers going on as though everything was dandy, bringing in big boxes of doughnuts and cookies and muffins every morning, bringing out birthday cakes each afternoon. And they'd stuff all this lousy sweet baked stuff in their mouths, to stop up the poison that wanted to come out.

By the time Ken's bail strike happened, most of my friends outside work were so sick of hearing my horror stories about SMAT that I just gave them a break and stopped mentioning it to them. The only place where I could discuss all the fear and tension I was witnessing at work was the coven. Dana was my most sympathetic listener, though she wasn't an active SMATter anymore; her husband had gotten so tired of it all he'd let her quit and get pregnant.

"Would you like to try the love cakes again?" Padraic asked one night.

I said I couldn't see how it would work, how would I get them to eat them? they tasted like they were full of chopped worms. He suggested there might be some other sort of magick we could try to make my coworkers all get along.

I just lost it then. I screamed that I didn't *want* them to get along, none of those SMAT people deserved any peace, they were all vicious and selfish and cowardly and I wished they'd just get it over with and kill and eat each other. I realized, in the silence that followed, that horrid as it was this might not be such an unpopular sentiment.

"We should do a spell to get rid of Ken," said Dana.

But we had taken vows to do no harm.

Nils said, "What's the harm?"

Dana said we should consider what Ken was doing to me and all the people at SMAT. Nils said yeah, and getting Ken fired would actually benefit Ken, since it would free him up to do what he really loved to do, which was apparently to hang around dirty old garages talking about himself to media people all day.

I asked them how they proposed to get the trustees to fire Ken, since other than murdering him that was the only way to get rid of him. Jude suggested you could feed the board hate cakes and turn them against him.

"That would actually work," said Nils. "Do we have a recipe for hate cakes?"

"No, just the love cakes."

"But wouldn't it make sense that you could reverse it somehow? Sort of a homeopathic effect."

"But I can't get the love cakes to work!"

Padraic brought up the subject of the missing ingredient. As I mentioned, it's a truism that when Witches write down their formulas, they always leave out one crucial ingredient, the catalyst that makes it all come together. That's a secret that's passed on from master to apprentice, so that fools and evil people can't get hold of the power.

"Give me the recipe," Nils told me. "Maybe I can figure out what's missing."

I wrote it down for him.

"There must be something we can do," Nils said, in his low soft voice. "You can't go around like this. You just hurt all over and you feel so ashamed and dirty, working for that man."

How did he know how I felt?

"I always knew you were a Witch," more than one person has said to me when they found out that I was. "You had that black cat."

But neither of the cats that lived with me then were mine. Joel and Casper both properly belonged to my ex-husband. I hadn't wanted to keep them, but he'd refused to take them when I'd made him move out, though he still insisted they were his and wouldn't let me give them away. And though I got along with them well and liked them we weren't particularly close. Joel was the black one. I would have hated to have had him as a familiar. To have had to rely on him as my intermediary with the spirit world would have been utter terror. He was a nice cat but a dim bulb. Having lived all his life in apartments, and having been raised by who he was raised by, he was completely cowed and denatured. Birds terrified him. You would give him a piece of steak or chicken and he wouldn't know what it was; he'd stare at it and bat it around. I once bought him one of those boxes filled with corrugated cardboard scented with catnip, that they're supposed to use as a scratching board. Joel never scratched it once, but he loved to sit on it. He'd settle his little haunches carefully along its narrow width, balancing himself with his forepaws, and sit there for as long as he could without falling off. He'd snarl at Casper if he tried to come anywhere near his darling seat. His favorite thing was to have you slide the box around while he was sitting on it. He would run and sit on it when he saw you coming, and look up with you with his big yellow moon eyes, hoping you'd give him a ride.

It always seems like when people have two cats there'll be a sleek, slim, twitchy cat and a fat, fluffy, relaxed cat. That was Joel and Casper, though Casper had his quirks. He loved to get on you and just stretch out and sink his claws into whatever you were wearing and start kneading, rolling his eyes back and purring like a tractor. Sometimes he'd bite down on you like a tomcat topping a pussycat. It used to make me very uncomfortable until Padraic told me it had nothing to do with sex, but was a sort of throwback to kittenhood cats went through sometimes where they pretended to be nursing again. It's true I'd noticed a couple of times Casper would look very interested when he was near me while I was undressed above the waist.

Usually Casper was very, very calm and languorous, except for

33

sometimes when I'd hear a wild scrambling sound in the bathroom. I'd run in and see Casper's little head poking up out of the dark bathtub. He'd be frozen in place, claws spread, a look of frenzied guilt on his face. Then he'd leap out and slink off past you and make himself scarce for a while.

If anything, these cats were a mystery to me. They were not familiar to me in *any* way.

I think this would be a good place to explain some things to you about why I am a Witch, and my personal beliefs about Wicca, so that there be no misunderstandings about it. I know that you are a fair-minded person or you wouldn't be reading this, and you may even know a few things about my religion; that Wiccans are not devil-worshipers, and so on. But there is still this monster movie image of Wicca that always needs to be pulled aside, whenever I come face to face with people, and I want to take care of that now. I want you to know what kind of Witch I am.

My friend Tamara used to love to go to psychic fairs, for the fortune tellers mostly. Since she knew I studied the Tarot, she always wanted me to do readings for her. I hadn't done many readings for other people (for one thing, I didn't have all the card meanings memorized that well yet), but I thought I could practice on Tam. And besides, I reasoned she would know how it was just me doing it, and not believe in it too much.

One of the things I've found out about cartomancy is that though you may get better and better at readings, it's the askers that really need skills. Tam asked questions that really frustrated me because they were always too specific. The cards can give you an overall picture of the circumstances surrounding a certain aspect of your life, but they were never intended to give yes or no answers to a question like, should I get my hair done a different way. I'd do a big twenty minute session trying to pull up the connections between the cards, scry out the story they had to tell, then ask her how does this relate to your question? what do you want to know? And what a letdown, to have tried so hard to envision the significance surrounding whether or not Tam should go to the drug-store and buy a lotto ticket. I finally told her not to waste my energy anymore, just to get a dollar and buy the ticket. Still, every time I'd go to see Tam, she'd ask, "D'jyou bring your cards?"

One day she wanted me to do a reading for her in one of the coffee-houses we always used to go to, for the atmosphere. So we were sitting there and I had my cards out, when a young girl came up and asked if I could do her next. I said yes, and when it was her turn I went ahead and did what I usually did, hoping I wouldn't make myself too ridiculous. I felt so ashamed, like an illiterate with a great book of wisdom in front of me I was ridiculously pretending I could grasp. I tried my best to tell the story the cards indicated to me, then asked the girl what her question was.

She told me honestly, plainly, as if I had every right to know: she was nineteen years old, and she had a baby. Not married, naturally. Her boyfriend and family hadn't let her get an abortion; they were Christian and very religious. Now she was stuck living with her family, and the boyfriend wouldn't do anything for her or the baby, and she wanted to go to college and was wondering if she'd ruined her life.

At this point I just forgot the cards. I told her look, when I was young, I did everything they told me to do. I went to college straight out of high school. I put off getting married and starting a family, and spent half my life in a drugstore or up on an exam table with my feet in stirrups so I could carry on some kind of a sex life in the meantime. I threw myself into my work and waited till I was thirty to settle on a husband. And he turned out to be a mad parasite, and my employers decided they'd save money by thinning out the more expensive staffers and threw me out on the street. And now I was nearly forty years old, all alone, with no savings and a bad job I might lose tomorrow. I told her, please don't think that you have to have some grand scheme in mind for your life. You could always go to college when the kid is older, having your babies when you're young and strong isn't such a bad idea, and how about telling Friend of the Court that Mr. Right-to-Life isn't paying his child support?

I think this girl really listened to me. It made me very uneasy. Just because I was grown up, and wearing a good scarf and dress, and had a nice fresh set of Rider cards in front of me, she acted like it was perfectly reasonable for me to know these secret things about her, and to tell her what to do and think about her life. I saw then how you could use these cards, and the honorary powers they bestowed on the person who carried them, to lie to people, convince them of any delusion, and take their money—any amount would be outrageous under these circumstances. I saw the face of evil then, what they call temptation. And my inclination was to pack up my cards and get out of that coffeehouse, and never go back again.

But Tam insisted we go back that night, and that I take out my cards again. And this time another person came up and wanted a reading. He was a bald man in a sort of sarong skirt, and he smiled like he was gentle and friendly. He had a bulldog face, that with the baldness made me think of the Great Beast, Aleister Crowley. That did it for me. I said maybe later, and dragged Tam kicking and screaming out the back way.

To trick people and be a magnet for weirdos is not a life for me. I am not a certified public Witch. My craft is my private observance. That's not to say I don't care enough to share what I know with others. If you come to me in genuine need, and I can do something for you on a practical plane, I will never turn you away. But my home is not a tent in a paranormal bazaar. I will never lie to anyone for my own enrichment or theirs. And if you need a psychiatrist, you'll be told so by me. I won't humor you. I never claimed Wicca was a substitute for competent medical or legal consultations, and you should never trust anyone who does.

Witches have always been known for carrying on the tradition of folk remedies, and there's nothing wrong with that; a lot of the million-dollar pharmaceutical products of today evolved from Wiccan herbals. Having said this, I should mention I am not a big fan of alternative medicine. There was a time in the earlier part of history where you went to the old wise one in the village when you had a health problem, and she fixed you up. Then the medical profession came along and in its fumbling authoritarian way ran the Witch doctors out of business. Organized medicine has its ugly side, and I understand that M.D.s are not gods—I drank beer with plenty of them when they were undergraduates—but if I ever get cancer or have a baby, I want to be in the hospital with every possible tube stuck into me. I don't see what automatically makes a midwife more trustworthy than a licensed obstetrician. Also, if you go to some homeopath and they turn out to be incompetent, what recourse do you have? At least doctors have money and you can sue them.

Of course I crave mystery; of course I love magic. What human being with an ounce of soul in her doesn't? But do you know what the most impressive magical ritual I have ever taken part in was? It was my wedding. My state-sanctioned marriage service in the Unitarian church. It was so utterly numinous. I've been with friends who got hysterical the night before their marriages, panicking and crying. But I was so ready to be married, I was so sure that I had chosen the right man (of course I didn't know him very well then), I was the calmest bride anyone ever saw. The night before the ceremony I sat with my friend who was baking my wedding cake, and helped her make fondant roses to decorate it with. And on my wedding day everything happened so easily. It was a beautiful warm afternoon, I got to my little hidey hole next to the ladies' room right on time, and all the people I loved were around me, waiting with me for the music to start. Suddenly I was just shaken by terror. Not what you'd think—I wasn't afraid of my groom (as I say, I didn't know him that well). It wasn't doubt about what I was doing. I quaked like a frightened animal because I could suddenly see very clearly the sacred nature of what I was just about to do. I felt that *it*, that thing they call God was watching, was aware of what was to happen, and would really be there to bless my groom and me. That's a terrifying feeling. "Bless," you know, is a word that's related to the word "hurt." To invoke any kind of a super-natural power like this should terrify you, there's no question; you ought to be in awe of it. People who play with sacramental power can do terrible harm. Look at what happened to me, with that marriage.

People think of Witches as telekinetic movers and shakers, and Witches themselves promote that image. But I'm very skeptical about claims that this spell or that rite can enchant or change matter. There's a fine line between what we can actually make happen, and what we can convince ourselves or others that we can do. My Tarot deck, for instance: do the archetypal symbols on these cards really draw on my psychic powers and give me paranormal glimpses of unforseen events, or are they just little doors that open into my very normal natural powers of psychological insight? We tend to see patterns in everything, even in utter chaos; that's the way our brains are built. When it comes to perceiving cause and effect in ritual magic, we love to deceive ourselves, almost as much as unscrupulous others love to do it for us.

Be careful playing with magic! You're entering dangerous territory when you cross the boundary between the simple celebration of Wiccan rites and actual sorcery. Everybody knows the story of the three wishes, where you screw up because you either don't think through what it is you're asking for, or you make a stupid wish you don't mean, and either way have to use up all your wishes unwishing the earlier wish. The point of the wish fable, as with all other great pieces of folk wisdom, is that the plan of the universe is too complicated for the human mind to contain and manipulate. Put it another way, it will always outfox you. So it's better to tamper with it in little, known ways, like heating a house with electricity or curing a headache with massage. This also is magic.

I once had an argument with Nils about this, when he was my sorcerer's apprentice. It was right after one of our esbats, and he had tasted more than his share of the sacramental wine, I think, and may also have been smoking something before he came that night: his eyes had that cloudy, pink look. He was so cute, very excited about an idea he had, about us offering ourselves as consultants to the police, the way professional psychics do. I told him I thought it was unethical for Wiccans to charge for their services. "You're such a *good* lady," Nils said, patting me on the cheek.

He had worked out this whole system that combined forensic science with sympathetic magic to create the perfect justice delivery system. For instance, if a woman was attacked by a rapist, you'd gather up a sample of his semen or a hair from his nethers and use it to put a hex on him; make the culprit impotent, or force him to smash his car into a wall. If somebody kidnapped a child, you'd cast a spell so that the kidnapper would go into a trance or do something stupid so that the child could escape. If you were dealing with a fugitive, why not fog his mind, make him think he was running into a hideout when it was really the state troopers' headquarters?

I told him that even if we knew how to make magicks like this—and I certainly didn't—there were other problems to be considered. Say that the woman who was raped, who you took the semen sample from, had a lover; how would you know whether you were hexing the man who harmed her or the man she loved? It's the three wishes problem. How can you hope to take control of a situation where there are so many complex variables?

Anyway, there is often a discrepancy between formal justice and actual human needs. I told Nils about something that had happened to me at work. One of the clerks had come to me crying. She said, "Do you know how to kill so no one can find out?"

(How had she known I was a Witch? I assumed Dana told her before she left. I myself was always extremely cautious not to discuss my religious practices with anyone outside Wiccan circles. But I wasn't going to ask this girl any questions, or turn her away; I could see she needed help.)

I had her sit down and explain. Apparently her sister had been brutally attacked by a sexual predator. This man, who had had other rape charges filed against him but for some reason had never been arrested, had been fired from a job as a cable television installer, but had managed to hang on to his uniform and I.D. badge. He had had his eye on the sister, found out where she lived and when she would be alone, and got into her apartment claiming he was there to fix her cable. He beat her and did every humiliating thing to her he could think of until he got tired and left her tied to the radiator, warning her not to tell anyone or he'd come back and kill her.

For a moment I really wished I had cultivated some kind of lethal supernatural power; the idea of a monster like this running around free was disgusting. But then looking at this young woman dropping tears on my desk, it was clear to me what I really could do for her, what she couldn't even articulate through all the anger and shock. She had a hurt sister; that was her concern. To think of the cruel things this man had done to her sister, that she would have to remember all her life: the idea that he might have permanently maimed her ability to enjoy making love, one of the few things that makes life tolerable for the young, must have been unbearable. I realized then what she really needed from me. I asked, do you think your sister might like some sexual healing tea? She said, what?

I went home on my lunch hour and prepared it. It's one of my best recipes, made with a base of raspberry leaves and English Breakfast tea; it's full of soothing and mending things, and tastes wonderful. I put it in a little blue canister with golden stars on it, and gave it to the young woman at work, with instructions on brewing it and a charm the sister could say as she drank it:

> *Tiger bites.*
> *Goddess will save me.*
> *Goddess must hold me.*
> *Goddess must heal me.*
> *Tiger must sleep.*

I never asked her how the tea worked for her sister, and she never told me. But a couple of days later she came to tell me she had more news about that evil cable man.

It seems that as he was about to leave the apartment building after having victimized her sister, one of her sister's neighbors noticed his uniform and asked him if he had a minute to fix his cable, too. The rapist said sure, repaired the broken cable box, charged him $40 and left him his name and phone number in case he ever needed him again. Which just proves, you don't have to be a rocket scientist to be a rapist. He was in jail now, and all the women he'd attacked were lining up with their lawyers outside the courthouse, waiting for a crack at him.

The reason Wicca is called a craft is that in your practice and study, as you gain spiritual wisdom, you also acquire skills. We don't call the practice of our religion worship because it does not involve making a show of fealty to any greater power that is outside ourselves. What we do is celebrate our lives in our religious service, and in the course of our everyday actions put what we learn into practice, for the greater purpose of living happily and well. Learning spells is not part of our religious observance per se as much as it is a discipline inspired by our philosophy, which is pantheistic, altruistic, and sensual. Healing is good, so you learn ways of healing and use them. Harming is anathema, something we just don't do unless specifically provoked. Whatever powers we choose to acquire, we always take care to counterbalance with the wisdom that gives us the choice *not* to use that power. This might not make sense to you, but it's a vital part of our philosophy. If the acquisition of magical power for its own sake is what drives you and excites you, you will lose the desire, and the ability, to make the distinction between what's beneficial and what's destructive; you will cease to be a true Witch and become something else. And don't think you know what *that* is.

There is a saying in Wicca, "Do what thou wilt, an it harm no one." Years ago the Satanists purloined this saying from us, shortening it to "Do what thou wilt." A typical, tragic example of Satanic distortion and misunderstanding. When you amputate those five words of empathy, of caution, what are you left with? Does it matter anymore whether you use your athame to cut up a cake for the love feast or to plunge into someone's heart? What happens to justice then? And what is human life without justice?

Most people do not believe that there is any difference between a Witch and a Satanist. They have Wicca and Satanism all mixed together in a big monster movie muddle. Or they think there are good Witches and bad Witches, and that the bad ones have black pointy hats and the good ones wear pink plastic crowns. Listen to me: Satanists are not Witches, any more than Presbyterians are Buddhists.

We call Wicca the Old Religion because it *is* an old religion, the oldest we know of in the Western world. Its origins are as mysterious as those of the Tarot; all we know is that it appears to be a survival of the pre-Christian religions of ancient Europe. It was suppressed by the Christians for centuries, both in the Old and New Worlds; a few brave wise ones carried on its traditions, mostly through oral transmission, and what written knowledge we have of it is almost certainly corrupted by bad scholarship and meddling fakers and con artists. But Wicca survives, if nowhere else, in our collective unconscious. There are elements of Wicca in nearly every known religion, including Christianity and its evil twin Satanism.

Wicca is a positive religion. It has survived more than one millennium without any formal organization, without oppressive rules

41

AR

or coercion, simply because it is so beloved of its devotees. Satanism, on the other hand, only exists where Christianity exists; it is no more than a deliberate negative reaction to Christianity. Christians, for their part, seem to some of us rather in love with the idea of Satanism; it gives them something to define themselves against, to make themselves look better in comparison, though it doesn't always work out that way. Evangelical revivals historically have a way of sparking a resurgent interest in devil worship.

The Christian-Satanic myth that Satan was a favorite angel of God who rebelled and left Heaven to found an alternate supernatural kingdom in Hell tells it all. The Satanist is a Christian driven crazy by the idea that God, who supposedly loves him, would set him down in a world where he is forced continually to sin in order to simply survive and be human, and then punishes him for it. This is why Satanists love sadomasochist gear like whips and black leather. These are symbols of the double-binding God they satirize in their Black Masses. You will never find an atheist Satanist; they all believe in God, and act like bad teenagers trying to shock their heavenly Father. Habitual criminals and sociopaths are attracted to Satanism because they feel they are outcasts from the human race. The truly good things life has to offer aren't available to them because of their sick personalities, so they force themselves to learn to take pleasure in horrible things, and to destroy any innocent pleasure others might have that they will never enjoy.

I could never follow such a hard path through life, trying to please some unappeasable god, or throwing my life away to spite him. The Wiccan way is simpler. It doesn't take any mental or emotional contortions to light a candle or weave a bracelet of herbs. All you have to do is love life, and try to do your best with it, that's all.

There was a type of woman you saw a lot of at SMAT. I don't really have a name for them, but you could call them I'm-not-supposed-to-be-here women. Really, how they even ended up in this town, with not one piece of batiked clothing or a Rieker sandal among them, was amazing. When they looked at me, they probably thought, now *she* belongs here. Not *me*.

Most of them were blonde, or tried to be, fine-boned, underweight and under 5'7", between the ages of 30 and 60. None of them were beautiful but all of them had the fine Anglo features that are conventionally attractive when presented the right way, with the right overlay of makeup. Even with their varied hair colors, they had the look that men mean when they say "a blonde." They wore close-fitting clothes in dramatic colors and high heels, everything chosen to show their "assets." They were all divorced but had remarried or had fiances, or said they did. They were ill-tempered and touchy, prone to boasting and rumor-making, and always on the lookout for ways to get away with not doing their work. They acted like what men like Ken think of when they think of "women."

I wasn't used to being around women like that, and they made me very uncomfortable, especially since I found them very hard to work with and almost impossible to socialize with. I'm thinking about Sharonne, one of my coworkers who I had a fair amount of regular contact with, because she kept track of a lot of the data I used in my publications. We got along well enough, and might have been friends, but that never really came off because neither of us could figure out how this could be done. For my part, I just found it hard to communicate with her in any but the most superficial way. I was always on my guard with her, just as I was with all the other women in the office like her. I need to feel a certain relaxation, a measure of trust in another person in order to really be friends with her, and all the Sharonne types were just too irritable. They were always picking at you and themselves and other people, being moody and mean, then not understanding why you pulled away.

I think what made these women so cross all the time is that they felt like they weren't in the real world at all, but were stuck in a fake one, prisoners of a sadistic and unjust fate. From childhood they had been led

43

to believe they merited certain rewards for their careful cultivation of their attractiveness: diamonds and furs and couture dresses, charge cards with no limits, gorgeous houses that got cleaned without their having to lift a finger. But where were their poolside afternoons, their first-class tropical vacations, their ten-day marathon love affairs? What the hell were they doing, having to WORK? It was outrageous, an injustice that should have shattered the universe.

They were thin, they wore high heels, they had breasts and bottoms and legs just the right size and shape. What went wrong? Where were the men they were supposed to get, the rich, adoring ones? Their current boyfriends and husbands had money, but not that much and they were tight with it; they wouldn't even let them quit their jobs at SMAT. What clothes and sports cars and vacations they had, they had to wheedle off their cheapskate men, or more likely buy themselves, which meant they were hardly the quality and quantity they'd expected. Where were the jewels and money, the servants and passionate kisses their thinness and big-breastedness and carefully put-together sexiness were supposed to have gotten them? All their fashion sense and modeling school deport-ment went only to decorate an ugly gray office full of gearheads. What monster had schemed to put them in the same pay grade as *me*, Marga-ret, the hippie punk beatnik, who drove a seven-year-old Volvo and didn't own a pair of heels over an inch high? Or put them in a grade below Santa, who wore glasses and barked, and weighed as much as three of them put together?

It made no sense to them. It was why they were so crabby, like people whose alarm went off during a beautiful dream, that they could never get back to as hard as they shut their eyes and tried. Though they hated it, these women were just perfect for SMAT; SMAT corporate culture wouldn't have been the same without them. For one thing, with-out having these seductresses traipsing around, the men who ran the place might have put their tongues back in their mouths and looked around and saw how stupid and ugly everything was, and how the place was being run into the ground. But these women loping around in their heels and tight skirts made them feel sexy and fantasize they were men of action and incredible brilliance and charisma, with jobs that gave them invincible power.

When I first came to SMAT, I was in pretty bad shape, which, again, is probably why they hired me; they thought I'd fit in. Sharonne battened on to me quickly. She was always complaining about her ex-husbands, which I realize now was a way to ease into my confidence, and get me to tell my own ex-husband stories. Mine always topped hers.

Sharonne's husbands couldn't keep a job; they were liars; they drank. Mine smoked. He didn't before we were married; he told me he'd been off them for three whole years. But by our first anniversary he was back up to two and a half packs a day. I felt very guilty, because I felt that I must have driven him to it. Whatever I'd done, though, I certainly paid for it. I mean literally. Right after he married me he decided to quit his job and start working on his first book, *Rough Cuts: The Encyclopedia of True Crime Movies*. This was pretty hard on me, since I wasn't making that much, not really enough to support two people, and not in the style he felt he was entitled to. And that book was quite expensive to do—he had to buy books and magazines and videos and a laser disc player and a new computer, take out-of-town trips to libraries and archives, do long-distance telephone interviews. And though he'd promised me he'd put down a deposit for a house for us with his first royalty check, what he actually made on that book was nowhere near what he'd told me it would be. The best year he had when we were together, his earnings were just about enough to pay for his cigarettes. Then there were the credit card bills I never saw and checks he wrote I never knew about until the letters and phone calls from collection agencies started coming in. Then I lost my job, and he threw my sewing machine through the wall. At least Sharonne wasn't one of the ones telling me I should have been more assertive with him.

But I soon began to shy away from trading divorce stories with Sharonne. It seemed to me she took a little too much glee in hearing about my mistakes, the losses and humiliation I suffered. That marriage had ruined me financially, destroyed my hope of having a family, and sent me into a near-clinical depression. It wasn't something I felt like making jokes about, or hearing other people kidding about. Besides, I

AR

hadn't broken up with my husband because I didn't love him. That's the way it is with me; even when there's reason to, I don't stop loving anyone.

Sharonne had been married twice. In her first marriage she had had a child, which lived with its father now in Washington State. It was strange how Sharonne kept wanting to talk about her husbands, telling the same stories again and again, as though it had just happened and she was still trying to get over the shock. But her last divorce was three years ago.

From what she told me, her way of living hadn't changed much since high school. She got up in the morning as late as possible, did her hair and makeup, put in her time at work, then went out with one of her boyfriends or went to the bar. That was about it. Looking good, putting herself out there on the market, biding her time till the right rich man came along. I think she was baffled that after three years of availability she hadn't had any serious takers yet.

"All I want is to meet a guy, get married, get knocked up and quit my job," she told me.

So you want more kids, I asked.

"No, I just don't want to work!"

One day we got a flyer through interoffice mail advertising a staff Halloween costume contest. "We oughtta go as *Witches*," Sharonne sniggered. I froze; what did she know?

Not everyone in the coven was as nasty to Nils as Padraic was. I think most of us were even fond of him, especially the older women. One of our covenmates, Laura, recommended him for a job at the university hospital, where she worked. I'm not really sure what he was doing before that, whether he was ever a student at the university, for instance. When we met I got the impression he was living with Chris, and that Chris was taking care of him. But by the time fall came, Nils was apparently living alone. At least, he told me he had his own room.

"So when are you coming to visit me?" he asked.

I never actually did. I don't usually socialize a lot with people in my coven, although I consider them friends; we do spend at least one evening a week together, and that's already more time than most friends can spare each other these days. I think it's important for us to have lives outside the coven, and since I am more or less in a leadership position I need to be careful not to dominate or monopolize my covenmates. We are a fellowship, not a cult.

But Nils, I think, was lonely. I never saw him with kids his own age, and it seemed strange that a good-looking boy like him never bragged about his sex life the least little bit. When Chris stopped coming to the meetings, Nils never talked about it or showed any reaction. I asked him once what was happening with Chris and he just said, "He lost interest."

I don't know if anyone I knew at that time was aware of how confused I was then about my relations with other people. Here I was, well into my thirties, and I still had so many adolescent attitudes. Like this fantasy I had that I was some kind of Dianic moon maiden who could foreswear the company of men and will myself into a pure, undesirous state of mind and body. Maybe because I didn't have the money and consumer goods that were supposed to belong to a person my age, I still thought of myself as a girl in many ways. I was only starting to realize that even though I felt sometimes fragile and unsure, people didn't see me that way at all. They asked my opinions; they *listened* to me. They saw me as strong. This had been going on since my late twenties but it was still strange to me. I was just beginning to understand that this had been the underlying thing that had made my marriage so nightmarish. My husband, you see, was six years younger than me, and though we were both in our twenties when we met and I thought of us as more or less being the same age, on the same level, he thought of me as an older woman, someone who ought to feel beholden to him. A mother, in fact, whose duty it was to give him all the love and good things his own birth mother hadn't. And also to take the rage he'd never before been able to express, when that other mother had failed him, and when (he thought) I'd failed him.

So there went my poor sewing machine, right through the wall! Well, if that wasn't enough to frighten me out of being a mother! let alone having any more men. But if I had managed to squash down my sexual self, in my misguided attempts to protect myself from any more scary experiences, I couldn't help the extrasexual longings that were aroused in me by the people around me. Especially with my covenmates, I had to give. I knew they needed me to care for them, to slip them a little of all that untapped milk of mother love in me.

Tam told me once that now that she was a mother she understood why children were so cute; it was an evolutionary necessity to keep you from slamming them against the wall. Nils had that appeal. He was small and soft, he had those big dark eyes and little boy bangs on his forehead. Even the manly things about him, his low voice, the hair on the back of his hands, made him seem younger, not older: precocious was what he seemed, not mature. Though he seemed perfectly capable of taking care of himself, he appealed to me in a way that made me want to take him on my lap, pet him and feed him. And I felt that he wouldn't mind this at all; he'd purr and sink his nails into me.

I was still almost positive then that Nils, if not entirely man-oriented sexually, at least must lean that way. I had grown used to thinking of all the men in the Gulo Coven as sort of safe. It played into my Diana-the-pure fantasy, that even while practicing the most sensually arousing rites of any religion on earth, I, the High Priestess, was beyond temptation.

He was always so cute and playful. He teased me by calling me Lady Myfanwy. I called him Puffin.

I spoiled him. I made his favorite poppyseed cakes for love feasts, I made him a cloak. This wasn't too special; I made cloaks for all my covenmates, using colors and textures and motifs that suited them, that they often picked out themselves. But the one for Nils was my very best. I made it in Dracula colors, with a black outside and red satin lining, specially weighted in the hem so it could be swirled in a dramatic manner. It was not particularly Wiccan, but it was his style and he just loved it.

I certainly didn't avoid him outside of coven gatherings. I had him over for dinner once, with Tam and her family (who hated him), and once I took him to a concert that my friend Murphy had given me tickets to, that I thought he'd like. It was a wonderful show, these Japanese percussionists, very athletic, who played these enormous drums half-naked. We had a great time. We went to the Cadillac Diner afterwards for milkshakes and fried mushrooms, and then went over to Word Up, which was still open because they were having a Midnight Madness sale. Of course Nils immediately made for the occult section; he was indiscriminately ravenous for any books that were the least bit witchy.

I was looking at some medieval woodcuts in a book about the European Witch persecutions when Nils came up behind me and snuggled against my neck. "Hell is the *best*," he said.

You want to be in hell, Nils?

"Yeah. It's sexy. You have people just where you want them."

He touched the page, as if to show me something on it, something among the bun-like bosoms and rough-cut buttocks topped by ox's-tails that should fix my attention.

"They're *trapped*," he said. "They're *naked*, they're *young*, they'll never get old. And they can never get away from you. At your mercy, totally. For *ever*."

Where Nils finally parted company with the Gulo Coven was over the skycladness issue. It made no sense to me why he was so insistent about this. You'd think that going naked in our climate and culture would be obviated. Even if you could withstand the chills and poison oak and mosquitos, the bottlecaps and broken glass and prurient peepers, there are other reasons you might not want to flash your body at the crowd. You might just not like the way your body looks; most people are ashamed to show themselves completely to other people, thinking, as we're all taught to think, that they're not beautiful enough. You might be wearing sanitary or prosthetic devices you'd rather keep to yourself, or have some unhappy memory connected with exposing your body that you'd rather not be forced to relive. Human reasons for evolving body coverings are just as sensible as those of clams and snails, and this should be considered before discarding them.

Nils thought we were prudish enough in the Gulo Coven because we hadn't done any sex magicks. Now there, I think, you're in a very gray area. Padraic and I were wary, at the outset, of getting sex freaks into our coven. Most sex magicks to me sound like excuses for weird games and orgies, even rapes. When you ritualize sex, and especially when you involve more than two people, or oblige people to take mind-altering concoctions to participate, you're introducing a potential for exploitation, and that we would never allow. I told Nils I thought the greatest sex magicks of all are created by two people in love with their eyes closed in delight.

"Too bad you're not more open-minded," said Nils. What he really was thinking about, he said, was not sex at all but the chthonic power of drawing the earth and sky into you, without man-made barriers between you. He said also we could create a stronger cone of power among us if our bodies were more intimately aligned. We agreed to talk about it early one evening before we began our esbat, so all of us would have a chance to express our views on the subject. Surprisingly, there wasn't much controversy. We more or less concurred that there was really no reason to wear our robes instead of something else, or nothing at all; it was just custom, and if anyone had objections they were not to be pressured into staying clothed. But most of us felt we would rather wear the robes. Padraic said he'd feel self-conscious, and that would offset any benefit of increased power from being skyclad. Nils said all right, but would there be any objection if he went without his robe? He hadn't brought it anyway. Of course, we said, do what you like.

As we got ready, Nils started taking off his pants. We were a little surprised he was really doing it. Some of the others told me later they thought he'd probably give up when he saw none of us was going to join him. But he behaved as though he were quite comfortable, and we politely tried not to make anything of it.

Nils was small in height, but you didn't think of him as little; he looked sturdy, in those shirts and pants and chunky shoes he wore. I didn't expect him to look at all delicate. But as he undressed, it was like the armor coming off, and this was the secret boy that had been inside all the time. His skin was so white. You could see right through in places, to the blue veins in his little masculine breasts. His body was smooth, hairless, all the way down to that startling patch where his legs met black and glossy, standing out against all that whiteness. I wasn't expecting how developed his arms were, little smooth muscles but hard and curved, and also his thighs, and when he turned you could see the indentations on the lower sides of the hips, curving inward, those little gripping places that I love so much on men. His nipples were so rosy, and his face was so serious. It made me wince when he took the athame and held it up in front of his chest. Think about handling a knife that way, with your breasts or penis bare.

He wasn't excited at first. But then, when we lit the flames and took up the chant, I saw the change. Everyone stared. It wasn't the size, though that was very respectable; it was the tension you sensed, the unashamed strength. My invocations went dry in my mouth. Though I kept guiding my eyes back to what I was doing, I couldn't stop looking at him. He was beautiful. I'd always known it; I'd never realized it.

He was very sweet afterward, laughing with us, tucking his revealed self back into his pants as we cleared up. But he just went home afterwards by himself, and the rest of us didn't go out together as usual, but split up and went home, too. I felt exhausted and very sad for some reason.

After that, he just didn't show up at our next meeting or any other. It was more comfortable that way, really. We all felt he was too young for the group, though we'd never wanted to exclude him; it had just always seemed we were too slow for him somehow, that we were holding him back, and who would want that? We felt more like ourselves now, though weaker without him. He'd kept us on our toes, like any outsider does.

That fall I spent a lot of my time preparing for our first sabbat in honor of Samhain, what the Christian world calls Halloween. I wanted it to be a night we'd all remember: glamorous, in the ancient sense of *glamour*, the charismatic radiance of spiritual strength. I asked Djanga if

51

she had any tips for me on how to celebrate this holiday. "Oh, you know, go to the Goat's Head and browse around," she said. "They usually have all sorts of special candles and crap."

Though I naturally go in places like the Goat's Head now and then for things I need, I don't like them much. The atmosphere of these places doesn't appeal to me—crystals and bad jewelry and aromatic oils that fade into tinted slop when you get them home. Also, when I'm in them I see so many books on the shelves that I disagree with that I feel like I'm entering into a potential argument with a thousand other minds just by scanning a few rows of spines. Honest Witches have to keep company with so much nonsense and charlatanism, at least in the marketplace.

Where I feel most myself, spiritually, is not in the Goat's Head but in the fabric store. My sensual self is naturally drawn to the sequins and feathers, but even a bolt of gingham can be exciting in its tight-wound state, with its unrealized possibilities. The mystery of the glass case with the skeletons of bridal helmets, the sizing in the air biting your eyes. The infinitely subtle spectrum of the thread spools always awed me. Think that there are actually that many colors, that there are women who master them. There's no more satisfying sound I can ever remember from earliest childhood than that thunk of the measuring machine biting the fabric, when I saw the cut point as it was drawn out onto the counter, and then the slithering snick of the scissors as it parted the cloth from its bolt. The beautiful accuracy of how those ladies cut the fabric, and on our own kitchen table how my mother cut so cleanly around the darts, with no mistakes, never creasing the tissue or running up against a pin, calmly, with pleasure in expertise, like a surgeon—that always thrilled me. I have never been so neat, though my seams have gotten straighter over the years.

I've loved the buttons always, the little cards on the wall in the notions nook. I worried about their fates, I wanted to give them all homes: the dull white round ones, the brass embossed shanks that seemed to have some European military origin, the little pale ducks and dinosaurs, all measured like music, 1/4, 5/8, 7/8. One of the things I inherited when my mother died was her button box, an old fruitcake can with the buttons left over from things she sewed, or buttons she bought just because they appealed to her, intending to use them some day, but that never got their chance. I cried over my orphan buttons when I first took them in, but now I have plans for them. I've already got the fabric, a gorgeous velvet, deep blue like the midnight sky. I'm going to make a Gypsy robe of it, and sew on all those buttons. And I will wear it at Beltain, and for blessing new babies.

I had a weird, sad feeling after our experiment with nude worship. I felt restless and dissatisfied, even at esbat time, usually my greatest time of relaxation and emotional renewal. The fact was I was missing Nils. I couldn't even have told you what our relationship was, but maybe because it was so interestingly vague I felt its loss so much more. Nils had a right to his own ideas, and we ourselves had a right to differ with him, so it was best we parted amicably. Still I felt bad. Guilty was mostly how I felt, as though I had rejected him, though he was the one who had left us, but even this I felt bad about. Maybe you've had the experience of someone you weren't interested in following you around, and then after you discourage him and he goes away like you told him to you feel angry, like, am I that cheap? you didn't try harder than that?

Anyway, I felt relieved the night he finally called me. "I've broken the code," he said.

I said what code. He said, "For the hate cakes."

He was very excited and pleased with himself, telling me all about it; it took three or four minutes before I could convince him I didn't know what he meant. "The love cakes," he said. "The hate cakes. To make the SMAT trustees hate Ken."

You have a recipe?

"*You* have a recipe."

For the love cakes.

"For the love cakes, yes, but the hate cakes too. It's the same recipe."

I apologized for being so slow, but what did he mean?

"All right," Nils said patiently, "what goes into those cakes, the love cakes? The ingredients."

I wrote them all down:

AR

Jiffy mix
eggs
milk
sugar
vanilla extract
Italian sausage
semisweet morsels

"Think about it," said Nils. "Is that like any recipe you've ever read in your life?"

I said I didn't get it.

"First of all, what is Jiffy mix? What's in it?" Flour, salt, baking powder. "So in other words, those are just the things you'd put in anything you'd bake. So you don't need Jiffy mix, to start with. That's just a psychological ploy, to throw you off." What? "So you feel dependent. Don't think, just use the mix. See, right there they're trying to make you think like a consumer, not like a Witch. That's how they control you. It's all mind control!"

I was beginning to understand a little. I said I was sorry now I'd bought that big box of Jiffy mix; what a waste. "No, that's okay, you can still use it," Nils said. "But think about what you're actually putting into that recipe. Break it down to its elements. Do you notice them mentioning butter or oil or shortening?"

Had I forgotten? I ran and got my spellbook, where I'd copied down Padraic's recipe. No, it didn't say it.

"That's the tipoff," said Nils. "That's the missing ingredient. You always use some kind of fat when you bake, right? It's basic cooking chemistry. That's what the Witch in you should tell you when you read this recipe.

"What clued me in," he said, really fast, excited, "was the semisweet morsels. It doesn't say anywhere these are chocolate chip love cakes. What these are are chocolate love cakes. You see? You melt the morsels and mix them in and that makes what? chocolate batter. That way you don't taste the sausage. It's like when my mom would make chocolate zucchini cake or put in prunes or pumpkin or some shit that's supposed to make it moist."

Of course! So you could use cocoa or baking chocolate, not just morsels. That would make it a lot cheaper. Of course, you'd need to add more sugar.

"Sure, the morsels are just a shortcut, like the Jiffy powder. That Witch that wrote that recipe must be the world's worst cook."

Well thanks, I said, if I ever need love cakes I'll know what to do.

"You don't need love cakes, you need hate cakes."

But I didn't have a recipe. "YES YOU DO!" Nils shouted.

At this point I felt a little testy, not to mention embarrassed and confused. I took a moment to cool down, then said, Nils, I'm sorry, but the Socratic method just doesn't work for me, will you please just tell me what you mean?

Nils apologized. "Margaret, I don't mean any disrespect," he said. "You have a wonderful Witch's brain in there. But they've put all these layers of oppression and depression and doubt on it all your life, to keep you from being free. You just need to clear it all away. Get rid of the slave brain and you'll see everything."

And I knew just what he meant then. I liked to think my work life and real life were separate; that wasn't true. The ugliness going on at SMAT was poisoning my spirit. My mind was weakening with pain, my energy was bleeding away. Was this the way for a Witch to dispose of her life?

"The board meeting's tomorrow, isn't it?" Nils asked

It was the day the trustees were slated to vote on renewing Ken's contract. "You know, they might not work, the cakes," he said. "But would it hurt anything to try it?"

All right, I said.

"Okay, we start on the premise that these love cakes are basically just plain ordinary chocolate cupcakes, with one weird ingredient, the sweet sausage, and that's the catalyst to spark the other ingredients. So you ask yourself. What makes the sausage the catalyst?"

Because it's meat?

"Yes, that's, ha, one thing."

Because it's Italian.

"Well, could be, yeah, but what else?"

It's spiced.

"What else?"

I couldn't think of anything else.

"Margaret, what is a sausage shaped like?"

Now I caught on, the typical Nilsian train of thought, the sympathetic magic. So you mean, I said, the phallus, the giver of life and sustenance, the muscle of love.

"All right. Now just think about that, and what, could you tell me, is the satanic opposite of this love sausage?"

You don't mean something that's, like, a vagina, I said.

"Margaret, *no*! You think I'm some kind of sexist?"

The satanic opposite of a sausage. I thought and thought. I couldn't imagine it.

"Well, don't worry," said Nils, "I know what it is, and I'm coming right over."

I really must be majorly depressed, I realized as I hung up and looked around my apartment. Usually I keep things picked up in case I have visitors, but when was the last time I had even felt like calling up one of my friends? How could I have let things go like this? The carpet was full of grit and fluff, the bathroom basin was going pink, the cat boxes were like a compost heap. I cleaned everything up as quickly as I could. I also managed to take a shower, fix my hair and brush the cats before Nils showed up. He looked a little tired. "Sorry it took me so long," he said, "I had to get something."

He showed it to me. It was a plastic peanut butter jar with holes punched in the lid, with water in it, and in the water were twitching, mud-colored things. Nils tried to give me the jar, but I couldn't touch it.

"I caught them myself," Nils said, holding them up to the light, looking at them, little glints in his round, dark eyes. "I went to that little pond near our meeting place, I got them there. I'll bet they've absorbed some of our power. What do you think?"

You caught them in the dark?

"Sure. I just put in my arm and left in there, pulled it out five minutes later, there they were."

Oh, Nils, how did you get them off?

"Just pulled them off."

I dragged him into the bathroom, took off his shirt, got some cotton and hydrogen peroxide and started rubbing it on his arm. I lectured him: Haven't you seen *The African Queen*? It's very bad to pull off leeches! They might leave their little mouths stuck in your skin and you'd get blood poisoning. You're supposed to rub them with sand or salt to irritate them and make them fall off of their own free will.

Nils was all bloody, and probably not at all as comfortable as he pretended to be. It looked like those little raw wounds would hurt. I fixed him up with bacitracin and bandaids, and then went to my medical dictionary and looked up blood poisoning. I had no idea what it was. I gave him my thermometer and told him to take his temperature every few hours for the next day or two, and go to the doctor if he felt at all funny.

"Now can we make the cakes?" he asked.

I told him there was no way I would cook those things in my kitchen. "All right, I'll do it," he said.

I felt so bad. Here he had gone to this trouble, actually used his blood, to get them for me, and it was all for nothing. It was a repulsive gift, that jar of worms, but I felt terrible rejecting it. Nils kept looking at me with those beautiful animal eyes, smiling at my squeamishness, wondering why I wouldn't just go along with it, but how could I do this? It was positively psychotic, the idea of feeding those things to the people I worked for.

"Yeah, let them play on your ethics," said Nils. "You're too good to do it to them. But look what they do to you. What have *you* been eating all these years?"

I was feeling sick to my stomach. Nils got me a glass of ginger ale, made me sit down on the couch, and put his arm around me, talking to me very softly.

Here I had a chance I might never have again to make a difference for the good. Did I want to take responsibility for letting the board subject everyone at SMAT to Ken for another year? How many people were going to lose their jobs because of that? How many people would get sick, or even die from stress? I believed in doing no harm; didn't I also have an obligation to help other people that I knew were being hurt? And was it really benefitting Ken to keep him on as managing director of SMAT? He obviously had nothing but contempt for the job; he probably only stayed there because his God's Family elder told him to. Think how he must feel, having to go to work every day and deal with a building full of people who hated him. It was obvious he didn't belong in that job; he just wasn't management material, and he must realize it and might even hate himself for it. Maybe that was what made him go around attacking little boys. If we released him from that burden, we might be saving his life. We might be saving his soul.

We wouldn't be doing anything to the trustees. Not a thing. They wouldn't have to eat the hate cakes. We'd just offer them to them and let them decide if they tasted good. It wouldn't make them sick if they didn't know what was in them. Probably it was no worse for them than what was in Italian sausage.

He brought me the jar again, opened it so the little things could get more air. "See," Nils said. "I didn't hurt them. I was very gentle with them. I didn't rip their little mouths off. Look how healthy they are. They had a good meal off me. I'm pretty tasty, you know. They're in a good mood, I bet they wouldn't even bite you if you held one. I bet you've never even touched a leech before. Here," he said, reaching a finger in, "want to try?"

I screamed. Joel ran under the sofa. Someone started pounding on the door. It was my neighbor; he wanted to know if I was all right. It was horribly embarrassing, me trying to convince him Nils wasn't my boyfriend, that he wasn't abusing me.

By this time, I was really shaken up. I told Nils, I can't do it, you do it.

"But that won't work," he said.

Why not?

"Because it's *your* hate, Margaret. If I made this spell, all that would go into it would be flour and animals. You've got to put in the passion, or it won't work."

I saw the sense in this. It made me agree. We'd assemble what we needed, do a ritual cleansing, and I'd say an invocation to clear away the bad spirits. For a moment, I was afraid Nils would want to do it nude. But he was clever, ceded the control to me, and my priestess self took over. I began to see this as a spiritual inquiry, an experiment.

I set the oven to 350. I melted chocolate in the double boiler, creamed some butter and sugar together, added the vanilla, then sifted in the flour, baking powder, and salt. I sprayed nonstick spray in the muffin tins. Then I sat on my kitchen stool and made myself watch the rest.

First he took my colander and drained the leeches. They squiggled around in it, panicked and disoriented. Nils reached for my food processor, but I said no.

So he waited till the struggling leeches tired themselves out, then put them on the cutting board and got my big carbon steel blade to chop them up. It was hard, they kept moving. He had to stop and sharpen the knife. They kept rebounding.

I had to help him saute them. There was an indescribable aroma, strangely savory. I realized what was the true missing ingredient: the fat off the leeches. It all went into the batter, and then the chocolate. He had chopped the little things so finely you would barely know they were in there. We put in a couple of handfuls of chocolate chips just in case.

It would have been better to have used little paper baking cups, to make them look more like cupcakes, but the only ones I had were old Christmas ones. Still, they came out of the pans beautifully, not one broken. I asked Nils, are you going to try one? "Not on your life," said Nils, with a wink. "I'm not putting a hex on *my* little sausage."

As the cakes cooled on their racks, I made up an orange buttercream. He had to do the frosting; I still couldn't touch the things. Then I had him put the cakes in a Tupperware box I used to keep old dry bread in for stuffing. "Are you going to chicken out on this?" he asked. "Am I going to have to bring these over to SMAT myself?" Yes, I said.

All the dirty things were still lying around, the bowls and utensils, the pans, the bloody slimy cutting board. I put on latex gloves and started putting them in a trash bag, just everything.

"If you're going to throw those out, I'll take them," said Nils. He left with my Tupperware box under his arm, with my cooking things clattering in the bag he carried.

Next day at work was a bad, tense day. Ken was hiding out in his office all morning with the door closed. I ran into Santa at the coffee machine. "Thanks for those cupcakes for the trustees," she said. "I can stash away those cookies I bought for next time. Your boyfriend's pretty cute."

I had chills and a sick headache that night. I couldn't even eat, didn't want to move, just laid on the couch with Joel and Casper. The next morning I had a sore throat and a low-grade fever. I hurt all over, like I was full of poison. My teeth chattered so much I could hardly talk when I called in. I tried to get Ken's message machine, but Santa answered instead. "It's just as well you're not coming in," she said. "We don't have a boss anymore."

Considering how little he cared for the job, Ken took losing it very hard. He made a big fuss, had SOS's lawyer threaten the trustees with suits until they agreed to give him a golden umbrella of two years' wages. A week after the settlement, a memo went around to all the staff announcing new changes in personnel policy. As of November 1, flextime would be eliminated. That meant everyone had to be at work at 8:30 and stay till 5, and we would now work a 40-hour work week instead of a 37 ½-hour one, though our salaries would remain the same. Until further notice, there would be a freeze on new hires and raises and nonmanagerial promotions. Also, the company Christmas party was canceled.

When I first came to work for SMAT, I was more or less a free-floating agent within the organization, not technically a member of any department; my only supervisor was Ken. But now Santa and the trustees were organizing a shakedown, designed to consolidate management and supposedly control costs. So for reasons I never was sure of, I was reclassified from public relations coordinator to publications associate and placed under the supervision of Brenda Zang, who was Sharonne's boss.

I had seen her around before, but she had never looked at me. That wasn't unusual at SMAT. Managers rarely had any more to do with workers than they had to. Also, you had to consider what a struggle it was for poor Brenda just to get herself through the day, let alone pay attention to anyone else.

It wasn't unusual to find people with serious emotional problems at SMAT. Unstable people tend to be drawn to places like that; they fit their temperament and world view. Anyway, the situational stresses of working there were enough to bring out the latent psychological problems in anyone. But as far as sheer volume of diagnosable pathological conditions went, Brenda beat everyone in the whole building.

When I got to know her, Brenda had been at SMAT for eight years. I doubt, considering the condition she was in, she would have been able to find work anywhere else. One of the older people told me when Brenda first came to work there she was quite nice looking. My god, then, what a hag she'd made of herself by the time I first saw her. Sometimes I think Brenda wasn't so different than the SMAT sex bombs, so obsessed with staying thin; being smarter and more desperate than the others, she'd just ended up trying too hard.

Brenda was five foot seven and weighed one hundred pounds. I know these things about Brenda because she told me herself, without my asking—Brenda was not at all inhibited in this way. I learned, for instance, that Brenda had anorexia-bulimia. "My digestive system is shot," she would often say. Sharonne used to tell me sometimes she'd been in the bathroom and heard Brenda gagging herself. I don't know if this was true or not, but I would often notice Brenda at office party buffets making off with enormous plates of chocolate cake or candy. Brenda tended to eat either three leaves of a very exotic lettuce or a pound of chocolate: no in between.

Even as thin as she was, and she was not a lot thinner than some of the popular fashion models then, it was hard to imagine Brenda looking conventionally pretty. She looked exactly like what an average American would think of when he said the word "Witch." She had a broken-looking nose, long wiry bleached-white hair, pointy yellow teeth, skeleton hands, and little stick legs with long skinny feet. She wore ultra-tight clothes, usually about two to three decades too young for her. "I'm a *big* girl," she used to brag; she was very proud of her breasts, and was always telling us she really didn't need to wear a bra. From the way they stood out on her chest like tetherballs hanging on a pole, I had to guess they were breast implants, chosen to fit the figure she must have had before her eating disorder took hold.

Brenda also told us about some of her other problems: panic attacks, tachycardia, hives. She also admitted to me once that she had been diagnosed with obsessive-compulsive disorder. I suggested she might ask her therapist if she could take Clonopin; I had a friend [Murphy] who'd said it had helped him a lot with his compulsive behavior. "Yeah, but it's no good for me," she said. "I went on it once and it made me gain weight."

Despite her problems, I think Brenda felt she was a winner in life. She had total discipline over her figure; no one could accuse her of being flabby. She had a boyfriend, a lawyer in New York, who she flew out to see two or three weekends a month. She had a top-of-the-line leased sports sedan, she shopped at the most expensive malls, she binged on the best gourmet foods and went to the same therapist as the daughter of a very famous local mystery writer. Not only that, she was a boss. So she was a success by practically anyone's definition.

She was sort of nice to me to begin with, perhaps because I was trying so hard to be supportive, friendly and nonthreatening to her. When someone you work with is that sick, you feel protective and want to shelter her fragility, even if she is supposed to be your supervisor and by definition stronger than you. And it seemed to me, at first, that Brenda was in a shaky situation. Unlike Ken, she didn't have the luxury of simply choosing not to do the work she had been hired to do; she *couldn't*.

Her poor starved brain and body weren't up to it. She was constantly losing and forgetting files, reports, appointments, her keys. Sometimes I'd notice her sitting in her office, motionless, staring at her hands or her computer screen; I'd look again an hour later and she'd still be there, not moving. Teaching her how I did things, what my duties were, was impossible; she barely knew the procedures for running her own department, which she'd been in charge of for over a year. My new fellow staffers, Sharonne and Hulga, told me they'd basically been figuring it out on their own.

This was what Brenda counted on: that we'd understand her situation, cover for her. "Look at that," she'd say, putting her trembling hand in front of your face. "See that? I haven't slept in a week." Well, what could you do? Just go on doing your job as usual. At least she didn't get in your way.

AR

I've always loved Halloween. It's my favorite holiday far beyond what I've ever felt for Christmas and birthdays. Because it's not a potlatch of smug or guilty giving, or about marking the passage of an artificially designated milestone in time, or having to get together with a lot of people you're related to but don't particularly care for. Halloween doesn't require anything of anybody. If you don't want to give out candy, you turn off your porch light. If you don't want to dress up, you don't. And if you are Wiccan, you go to your sabbat celebration not because some god is watching you and will be mad if you don't show up, but because you just don't want to miss it. Samhain/Halloween is a jubilee for so many things: the gladness of being in this world, the wonder of thinking about the next, revelry in the richness of the harvest, and thankfulness that you have enough to survive the coming winter.

I always remember seeing Djanga on one of the television morning shows, saying, "Halloween is our New Years' Eve. You know how on New Years' Eve you dress up in your best clothes, to look rich, to symbolize the wealth and good fortune you hope you'll have in the New Year. That's how we dress on Halloween. We dress like what we want to be. That's why we don't dress up like ghosts!"

All my life I've loved fancy dress. I loved my wedding dress, I loved my bridesmaid's dresses, I still have all of them. Every time I walk past one of those boutiques on Main Street that cater to the local society women, and see all those beautiful beaded and batiked gowns in the windows, I think, wouldn't I love to live a life where I could wear clothes like these? Of course I wouldn't want to do the things I'd have to do to get them or put up with the people that went along with them, but a really gorgeous evening dress is my favorite work of art. Glitter brings out the magpie in me. If I had really followed my urge for it, I would have lived much differently.

For my first official Samhain festival, I decided to take Djanga's advice and costume myself properly. I made myself a gown of emerald green satin, bias-cut, with straps fashioned out of an antique paste diamond necklace. Then I dug out some opera-length gloves and satin shoes (the same ones I wore at my wedding) and dyed them to match. It took a little nerve to slink myself up like this, twenty years after my senior prom. But when I looked at myself in the mirror, over my rhine-stone shoulder, I thought: come on, you've got a few years left. There are in fact very few young, bony women who can successfully carry off an evening dress like this. You need a little ripeness in your shoulders and bosom.

I wore my Emerald Fantasy to sabbat on Friday night, and then again on Saturday when I went to a party with some of my friends. It was wild. We disco danced, bobbed for apples, drank something called a French Whore and got absolutely ridiculous. I thought: this is the rea-son why transvestites love to dress like this. You never feel better when you're in clothing that absolutely gleams. You can knock down the world. It's POWER.

My friend Tam got me to invite her to one of our esbats, but she didn't even end up staying for the whole thing. "I don't know, I was expecting something sexier," she said. Tam was raised Romanian Or-thodox, and I imagine after you've been in one of those big, gorgeous, established religions, a little Wiccan coven doesn't seem like much. Still, she asked me once if we had any programs for children she could take her kids Larkin and Amis to.

Why don't you take them to Steve's church? I asked. Her husband Steve was a Quaker.

"They make me uncomfortable," she said. "Too much peer pres-sure." She had an opinion on every religion. Jews were bondage freaks; Moslems were pod people; Zen Buddhists were passive-aggressive; any-one who grew up Lutheran ended up either agnostic or insane. A couple of times she tried going to the Unitarian church with me, but later she told me she hadn't felt she belonged there either. "Unitarians have to be too effin' nice," she said.

We had people participating in our coven who had children, but they had never asked about including them in our practices. For one thing, we held our rites at midnight, which would have been impossible for young kids. For another thing, Wicca is just an adult thing; the rituals would simply not be relevant to them. I supposed you could have a Sunday school for those who were too young to become initiates, but then again why? I didn't think it was necessary or desirable to indoctrinate young people in Wicca. Let them observe their parents and how the Wiccan way of life went for them, and decide for themselves whether or not they wanted to follow it too. I thought the proper age for an initiate would be no younger than seventeen, and probably older, considering that it takes a considerable amount of maturity, stability, and courage to be a Witch. Nils had been the youngest person we'd ever had in our coven, and he was twenty-two.

Anyway, a true Wiccan is born, not made. I always thought Larkin might make a wonderful one; he had the taste for theatricality that all the best Witches have. When he was about four, for instance, he was totally obsessed with pirates, but it wasn't enough to be read to about them or pretend to be one; he had to actually, physically, transform himself to fit his fantasy. At one time he owned three complete pirate outfits: a bandana-and-eyepatch one, a Jolly Roger hat-and-eyepatch one, and a Captain Hook (I made him that one). He loved the hook. One time he wore it when Tam and I took him with us to the mall. I noticed all these people we passed staring at him like, oh that poor little boy!

The question of tradition is a matter of much discussion in the American Wiccan community. There's a very strong Celtic influence among many of us, mainly because so many of the most influential modern Witches, Gardner and Leek and so on, were British. I know this strain runs very strongly in Padraic, and even though I suspect the last little bit of Celtic blood in me was probably drawn out some time ago for a cholesterol test or a Red Cross drive, it influences me too. There's something very compelling about the British Pagan way, their deep, familiar affection for animals and trees and plants and waterways, and their sensible relationship with the Little People. They have a healthy respect for the supernatural beings who live in their houses and gardens and woodlands, but no real fear. Probably because they've lived with them for generations and understand their ways. So when a British Wiccan visualizes a Horned God, it's in a very different context than how we American Witches would.

We Americans really have no parallel to the English faerie folk, the pixies and brownies and elves and leprechauns who trade tricks with humans and reward them for kindly behavior, or the mournful specters who rattle chains in their ancestral manors. We have Bigfoot and extra-terrestrials who kidnap and rape us. Our ghosts are sadistic sociopaths who chase us out of our homes on threat of death. Except maybe for the Native Americans, none of us have been here long enough to really make friends with the otherworldly beings we cohabit with. So the American Horned God is not at all the same as the British one, who hunts with a good will to bring nourishment to his people. He can't be that to us, because of what America is and what we are, we wild, angry people who hate to be cared for, and won't care for anyone. Our Hunter God is vicious and cruel, and his horns are pointed at us. He hunts us down; he batters and breaks us. Though it's Wiccan tradition, I never invoke him in any of my rites. He looks like Satan to me.

AR

I have no idea why Santa insisted on calling herself Santa. Her real name was Norma Santamaria Morton. I realize that's a slightly unusual name, but is being known as Norma any stranger than calling yourself Santa?

It may have been that like most people with an eating disorder, Santa had a distorted self-image. In some ways, though, she presented herself as beautifully as any woman might. She wore suits and dresses in soft pinks and greens and whites that looked smashing with her pale skin and coppery hair. If she had weighed 110 pounds instead of 300, she would have made every other sex kitten in SMAT curl up and die in envy. But something had happened to Santa that had frightened her so badly, made her feel so small that she had to make herself big, just to reassure herself she wouldn't disappear.

You know that when a child has been maltreated in some profound way she will never forget as long as she lives, she eventually comes to a turning point in her life where she has to decide how to cope with her unbearable experience of human cruelty. She has three choices: to destroy herself, to destroy other people, or to resolve to make sure no one else will ever suffer the way she has, if she can help it. You could see in the set of Santa's jaw, by the way she looked at anyone who wasn't in authority over her, which way Santa had chosen to go. This woman was dangerous.

You would hear her in her office with Brenda or one of the other compulsive gossips at SMAT, just roaring away, and you'd know nothing could make them laugh like that except something unpleasant about somebody else. But you never heard anybody say, "I heard Santa said." Santa wasn't a rumormonger. She maintained nominal friendships with select contacts like Brenda, high up enough not to be demeaning to her status, low enough to be eager to please her and proud to be one of the few she smiled at. But it wasn't just the prospect of malicious fun that made Santa want to know all the dirt on everybody below her at SMAT. She was collecting.

"Don't you feel great, now Ken's gone?" Dana asked me once. I smiled, but I didn't know. Things were quieter, but not safer.

I was once told by one of my school counselors that I had a problem with authority figures. That's true, and not a bad thing at all in my books, but it made for some tension in me when I realized I was now an authority figure myself. Here I was, never having been in charge of anything before, a High Priestess in charge of a whole coven: planning the rites, embroidering the altar cloths, offering cups of tea and a warm, tear-absorbent shoulder to my covenmates when they needed it. And here I was initiating people into Wicca, when I had never even been initiated myself.

The problem of initiation never even occurred to me until I was asked to do one. My first official initiate, Jude, knew it wasn't a question of being made a member of the Gulo Coven, because to me and Padraic she belonged simply because she'd been called to join us by her own inclinations. She said she thought of it as a personal rite, like a marriage, to celebrate her commitment to the coven. I think that's as it should be.

After researching how other covens handled initiation rites, we followed our usual pattern, borrowing what appealed to us from what had been done before, and then inventing the rest, according to our own inclinations. There was some validity to this approach. I do hate the bad poetry and false Ye Merrie Englande stuff you find in most published Wiccan literature. Why pretend you're sixteenth century Britons when you're second millennium Americans? As far as weeding out the authentic Wiccan traditions from the contemporary made-up ones, that seemed futile to us. We found that what mattered to us wasn't whether it was "real" or not, but simply whether or not it worked, and most importantly whether or not it suited us. Reading through the literature on initiation, for instance, I liked the tradition of washing the initiate in salt and perfume. Everybody can respond to the symbolism of emerging from a warm, fragrant bath reborn, with new resolve. But I couldn't accept the gesture of binding the person hand and foot and asking her to swear loyalty at the point of a knife. It seemed like some sort of gang initiation. Padraic and Jude agreed.

But later I came to understand how dangerously naive we were, taking such a casual attitude towards such a vital sacrament as Wiccan initiation. We didn't understand the underlying significance of the knife and the rope; that's why it was so easy for us to discard them. But rites of passage aren't meant to be pretty and reassuring. They are more than an affirmation, an easy vow; they are a total transformation of one's being.

It's not the marriage vows that make you married, but paying your fee and taking that horrible class on sexual infections, and hiring the minister and the hall, and inviting everyone to come watch you, and most of all signing that paper that says you are obligated, and willing to pay for what you're getting into.

We still had to learn that in taking someone into our fellowship, there was something desperately serious at stake: the security and safety of not only the coven itself, but every one of us in it. How ridiculous not to even think of that, given how much I knew of Wicca's history. A coven must be a secret place, not because of exclusivity or shame (I hope I've made it clear that nothing has been done in the Gulo Coven that needs hiding), but because of the irrational, vicious persecution that every known Witch has had to suffer. To be a Witch means either to stay cautiously unknown to the world as a Witch, or to risk everything. If someone let it be known to the outside world who we were and what we were doing, what civil rights law would have protected us? We were on rocky legal ground; the Gulo Coven wasn't even registered as an official religion (a situation that was later remedied, I assure you). We could lose our jobs, be evicted from our homes, be slandered, harassed, even physically attacked, and our community, our courts, and our government would feel no obligation to protect us.

Here is my advice to all priestesses: You may know who you share your rites with, but *you don't know them*. Make any sentient being who sets a toe near your magic circle swear, on pain of slow, ragged flaying with a salty blade, to never divulge the identities of any person connected with your coven, to never expose the location of your rites, and to never discuss the Craft with anyone, however dear or sympathetic, without unanimous prior approval of the coven. This is one of the old traditions, will you nil you, you had better keep.

Just up the road from where I lived was Zooty Farms. It was hard to remember that it hadn't always been there, that the great, profitable Zooty empire had had a very humble beginning as a rich boy's summer pastime.

There was a time around the start of the seventies when people were sick of machine-made, synthetic food and wanted desperately to eat something real. There were about six restaurants in town that specialized in vegetarian, macrobiotic, and general Adelle Davis-style health foods, a couple of organic food cooperatives, and at least one natural bakery. I don't know whether Dave Baumgardner really ever bought into this whole wheat way of life, but he certainly saw there was a demand in town that needed a supplier. Here were all these hippie university students, and school kids from the suburbs roaming around town pretending to be hippie university students, with hungry bodies and sweet teeth and an urge to feed themselves on something with a little countercultural style. So Dave came up with Zooty Cakes, a sort of underground satire on commercial snack cakes, the Twinkies and Hohos and Little Debbies and Moon Pies and Devil Dogs we'd all eaten as kids. Instead of being wrapped in slick cellophane, the original Zooty Cakes came in brown paper wrappers printed with cute Crumb/Shelton-type cartoon writing and drawings (now very desirable collectibles). And unlike the machine-tooled-smooth, cookie-cutter corporate snack cakes they were a reaction against, Dave's cakes were appealingly irregular, handmade-looking. They used refined sugar and flour, not exactly whole foods, but the general idea fit the concept: there were real strawberry pips in a Strawberry Thrill, and you could smell the zest in the Lemon Rush (not fake lemon-colored, but white tinged with bakery brown, like a real live cake). They advertised themselves as containing "No Plastics, No Preservatives, Only Love," and that worked out because from the very beginning Zooty Cakes never went stale; they sold very well.

At first you could only get them at the food coops or the Sunflour Bakery, and even though they eventually penetrated the "straight" commercial markets like party stores and supermarkets, for a long time you could only get them on the funky side of town. Then, in the eighties, when you would have thought Zooty Cakes would have died out along with black light posters and the Furry Freak Brothers, Dave gave them a huge unexpected push. Suddenly there were TV ads and billboards and T-shirts (not the kind you bought at the Sunflour Bakery; the kind you bought in T-shirt shops at the mall), and the hippie-dippie cartoons were out and a quarter-million-dollar logo was in, and the brown paper got folded away forever and the Cakes, now form-molded and predictably bumpy, showed through embossed cellophane. Right before the millennium, even though local progressives had been boycotting Zooty products for years by that time, Zooty Cakes were the second biggest selling snack cakes nationwide. So millions of American children ate them as their meal of preference at breakfast or lunch, and often both.

And no longer pretending to be a shaggy preservative-free home-spun entrepreneur, Dave could relax and let the privileged megalomaniacal bastard in him shine through for all to see. He'd quietly bought up acres of land on the edge of town during the recession when people were losing their farms, and like a fat Walt Disney erected his dream palace there. The world headquarters of Zooty Ltd. was always meant to be located there on what was now called Zooty Farms, but Dave had other ambitions for that enormous property. It was to be a nature preserve, an entertainment and education center for Zooty employees and the business community at large, a cultural complex, a temple of the glory of Caesar Caligula Baumgardner.

A lot of things that were meant to happen at Zooty Farms never came off. The theater and arts center, one of the most ambitious and talked-about ideas in the planning stages of Zooty Farms, never came about; it mutated into a sort of convention facility that got rented out for management seminars. There has always been a very active arts community here in town, though never a very wealthy one, and a lot of people were looking forward to having Dave's patronage. But another competitor crowded out the others who vied for a bit of Dave's wealth, and that was God, or at least his Family.

Dave's involvement with God's Family went back almost to the beginning of Zooty Ltd.'s first serious commercial outings, which was right when God's Family was first getting started. It was a freaky little friendly group then, and Dave, who despite his natural capitalism may have felt uneasy about becoming just another executive predator, probably liked the idea of joining up with them, as an alternative to the Big Church he was raised in. No one thought anything of it; being a Jesus Freak was thought of as a sort of sweet, apolitical thing back then. But as God's Family grew bigger and stricter and meaner to outsiders, Dave started throwing his weight around too, and considering how big he was, he bruised a lot of people.

You heard things. Apparently Dave was known to be very rude and arrogant, which got him excluded from local society in a way that was very abnormal for someone in his position. This was believable, judging from the sort of quotes from him that got printed in the paper (not the *Press-Dispatch*—that's always been very conservative and pro-Dave—but the major out-of-town dailies and national newsmagazines always seemed to get a kick out of making him look like a creepy pig). Brenda told me the reason the performing arts center idea never happened was that Dave insisted on preapproving all the projects himself, and was censoring everything. Like he wouldn't let them do *The Threepenny Opera* because it was written by a Communist, and he canceled a dance troupe because he thought the men's costumes were too tight in front.

You may have heard about working conditions at Zooty because of the lawsuits (the fudging of overtime pay, the dress code that was only enforced with women employees, the never-hire, always-fire policy for homosexuals), but I heard more intimate confidences from people who used to work at Zooty headquarters. People were always leaving there in droves; some of them even ended up at SMAT, which shows you how desperate they were to get out. So Dave was never a loved person in town. It must have been awfully lonely for him. This might have been why he started the Christmas lights, to make the people come love him.

The nature preserve, another one of those big promises Dave made when he took over that fat parcel of prime land, never appeared; the closest thing was a little park that more or less closed up when they found out none of Zooty's employees wanted to spend their Saturdays on Dave's territory. So, if you went into Dave's office in the executive compound, and looked past the desk where Dave sat eating and screaming at

AR

people all day, what you'd see through the floor-to-ceiling window be-hind him was a big ugly heap of dirt. Someone must have worked up the courage to point out to Dave that this was not the most flattering setting for himself. So, he had them go out and plant grass and flowers. He paved the little private road that ran through the old field, and had some tree transplanters uproot some beautiful old maples from the outlying countryside and shove them into the Zooty grounds. But all this expen-sive greenery must have still been too dull a backdrop for Dave, because he called a big press conference, and announced that he had a holiday gift to give all his friends and neighbors (and, presumably, the Edison Company): an electric tribute to Jesus along Zooty Parkway, which would be free and open to the public all through the holiday season, beginning at dusk on December 1.

This was supposed to be the biggest Christmas light display in the world, or so I overheard people saying, though I tried not to. At the time they were first publicizing the light show, I was so anti-Baumgardner I deliberately avoided reading about it or listening to the TV and radio reports hyping it. This turned out to be a very silly mistake.

December 1 that year fell on a Friday. I thought nothing of it; it was just another esbat night to me. It was a beautiful late autumn evening, mild and crisp and starry, and as usual on nice nights I just assumed that we'd meet in our usual clearing. As was my custom, I left a sprig of juniper in my mailbox slot so that anyone who came to buzz my apart-ment (where we met during bad weather) would know we were having our esbat in the woods. I thought I might be coming down with a cold, so even though it wasn't that chilly I wore two sweaters and my winter boots. It turned out to be good that I did, because I had to wait an hour and a half before my first covenmate showed up. Only three people managed to make it to our meeting place that night, and they were so tired and mad we barely got through the rituals. They were all ready to strangle Dave Baumgardner with his own electrical cords.

"You should have seen that goddamn road," Tim told me. "It was backed up all the way to the freeway. It took me all night just to get to Silvery Road, and I had to take a detour and go way the hell out to Bittenburg Township on those crappy back roads."

Zooty's publicists had done their work well. Every idiot within a hundred mile radius and his or her dog had driven every car they owned to Zooty Farms to see Dave's light show. Dave apparently hadn't even considered the traffic problem his little seasonal entertainment might cause. This is after all just a small college town in the middle of the country, with mostly two-lane roads. In fact, aside from a few unpaved back roads, the only way to get to Zooty Farms happens to be by the main road into town (which happens to also be the only way to get to my apartment without breaking your axle). Dave hadn't cared to consider how the increased flow of cars into Zooty Farms might slow down local traffic, or how visitors to the light show, having made their way along the loop of Zooty Parkway, were supposed to find an exit point onto the main road when that road was totally constipated with cars trying to get *into* the loop. Commuters couldn't get home; delivery trucks were stranded; ambulances had to go cross-country. We Witches were very bitter. All this hellish mess because of some Christian show-off. "I think it's time to hate-cake that fat fascist," said Jude.

And we weren't alone in thinking this. There was a big faceoff at the next city council meeting. People demanded that Dave's Christmas lights be banned as a public menace. But the mayor and council, much as they hated Dave, argued that it was a freedom of speech and religion issue. You couldn't prevent Dave from having a Christmas display on his own property. Not on legal grounds at least. There were of course other, more efficacious methods, but the mayor and council members cannily savored these in quiet, planning for the future. For now the best they could do was make Dave hire guards to direct traffic in and out of the light show. Dave refused to consider closing down his show voluntarily, and announced he was planning to make it an annual event. "If the honchos of this city don't know what the true meaning of Christmas is, I do," Dave told the media microphones.

Christmas displays were always provocative issues around here. One of our previous mayors always insisted on having a nativity scene in front of City Hall every year, no matter how questionable a mixing of church and state it was; he didn't care who he offended. It was an ugly old nativity scene too, such an eyesore; everybody hated it. I think the mayor kept foisting it off on us just out of spite. It became sort of a joke. Kids would tip it over or rearrange the animals in tasteless positions. Once somebody stole the baby out of the manger and replaced it with a cardboard dollar sign.

I myself really don't mind how they celebrate Christmas. After all, the Christians snitched the best parts of it from us Pagans: the glorified, gift-giving tree, the singing and feasting and merriment. The idea of a festival of lights in the darkest part of the year even makes medical sense, if you consider how many people suffer from seasonal affective disorder. So Dave had the right idea, but as usual he was obnoxious and heedless and squashed everyone flat as he rolled around getting his own way. He was just asking for it.

Bilbo was one of the caretakers in my apartment complex who I'd struck up a friendship with the summer before, when the old air conditioning unit in my closet caught fire. He was a cheery little guy, about twenty-five, not unintelligent but a classic burnout. I had the feeling he'd been given this job through his connections in some sort of recovery group. Like me, he loved movies and we were always asking each other if we'd seen this or that one. He loved the kind my ex-husband wrote about, like *Deranged* and *The Honeymoon Killers*.

It was the week before Christmas, not long after Baumgardner's showdown with the city council, when Bilbo came buzzing at my door. "Hey, Margaret," he said. "Want to come down and see my lights?"

I had just gotten home from work and was about to fix dinner. It was already pitch black outside, the way it gets around the winter solstice. Bilbo's apartment was right around the corner from mine; like mine, it was a second floor apartment with a glass doorwall opening onto a little balcony. Probably because he wasn't a paying customer but a live-in lackey, his view wasn't as nice, just a parking lot and the back of the rental office. Bilbo took me around to where his old rusted-out sedan was parked. Nils was standing there, in his usual black t-shirt and no jacket, even though his breath was coming in frozen puffs. I had had no idea he even knew Bilbo. "Ah, my lady," he said, smiling his sweet gentle smile, putting his arms around me and rubbing my shoulders, as though I were the cold one.

Bilbo was pointing, grinning, with all his bad teeth wetly reflecting the twinkling lights above us. I looked up. There was a big sort of black wagon wheel thing tied to the iron grille around Bilbo's balcony. Attached to this wheel were several strings of red fairy lights, making the outline of a huge circle. Inside this circle was a five-pointed upside-down star, the pentagram, the bad sign, the mark of the horned god.

This was not the inept gesture of somebody who just didn't know how to make a proper Christmas star. This was deliberate. In the patio window behind and above the wheel were lights spelling HAIL in dazzling gold-and-white twinkles, and under that, in red-orange bulbs so big you had to have been able to read them from the university hospital complex up on the hill across the road, was the word SATAN.

He can't have that up there! I yelled.

"Sure he can," said Nils. "If Dave Baumgardner can have his lights so can Bilbo."

But he *owns* Zooty Farms! This is an apartment!

"Just let 'em try anything. He's not the only tenant with a light display. What about that lady over there with a Mary statue on her porch? This is just another religious symbol, what's wrong with that?"

I tried appealing to Bilbo. Couldn't he see this could make trouble? And not just for him. "Yeah, for *you*," said Nils.

I had never told Bilbo about the Gulo Coven and my being a Witch. I didn't want that information spread around, certainly not around where I lived. Nils should have known this. And I certainly didn't want to be connected with this sort of nonsense. People were slow about subjects like Satanism; they wouldn't get the joke.

"It's not a joke. We're serious," said Nils.

There was a smacking crack, and then a rattle of cracks. Someone had a beebee gun and was trying to shoot out the lights. The patio doorwall to Bilbo's apartment shivered to bits and the lamp went out. Angry male shouts echoed over the parking lot, then the gunman banged away at the lights again, managing to knock out the string that spelt HAIL. We ducked behind the car. Nils held onto me; I felt him shivering, but he smiled at me like, isn't this the most fun?

As soon as there seemed to be a cease fire and we dared move again, I took off my sweater, made Nils put it on and then ran back home.

AR

About half an hour later, someone buzzed my apartment. "Police. Could we come up and talk to you for a minute?"

I had to tell them what I'd seen, which wasn't really much. I hadn't paid attention to where the shots were coming from; it might have been from behind the rental office, or maybe even from one of the other cars.

The cops drew closer in and changed the subject. Was I aware of any Satanic cult incidents in this area? Had I heard any reports of missing pets or animal mutilations? Was I, personally, involved in any kind of occult activity?

"Notice you've got a black cat here," said one of the cops, nudging Joel with his boot.

That night I called Djanga. I was so unnerved, but she knew what I needed to hear and was very reassuring. "As long as those friends of yours didn't talk too much, you're probably all right," she said. "Those cops probably just took one of those Satanic crime seminars and they're all excited. What a couple of Nazis! Do you go 'round calling *their* religion an 'occult activity'?" I asked if maybe I ought to cancel my coven meeting that week, if maybe we should go underground for a while. "No, don't you dare," she said. "Don't let them get the better of you—you just go right on. In fact, if you don't mind, I'd like to sit in this week."

As it turned out, we had to meet indoors anyway; it was a miserable night, slick with freezing rain. But Djanga managed to make it anyway, and we had a wonderful time. I asked her what she thought of our ceremony. "Well, it's pretty different," she said. "There's a definite Radical Faerie influence. You made a lot of it up yourself, didn't you?" But she said that was all right, that so many covens were practically like Creative Anachronism societies or folk dance classes, they were so arcane, and modernizing the rites didn't hurt a bit. It's true that one of the satisfying things about being a Wiccan practitioner is that there's practically nothing to get in the way between you and the actual celebration of your religion: no pomp, no property, no sacred texts, and no little dictators from World Headquarters running around censoring and excommunicating everybody who deviates from the script. "The wonderful thing about Wicca," Djanga told me, "is it's self-correcting. *It* lets you know when you've gone out of line."

I ran into Bilbo a couple of days after the shootout. He was in a pretty good mood, so I said I guessed he hadn't been fired. "Na, they just made me take my lights down," he said.

I asked him how he knew Nils. "Oh, he's always around here. We're plannin' another light show."

Here? "Na, at the place he lives at. His landlord said it's okay long as we pay the electricity."

And they did it—and did it get noticed. It even got on the cover of the *Press-Dispatch*, in color, what they could show of it. I know what the whole thing really looked like, because Nils insisted on picking me up on Christmas Eve and driving me there to see it. It was actually quite artistically done. The centerpiece of the lawn display, which the *Press-Dispatch* photographer had been at pains to obscure, was a plywood board, motorized somehow so it moved up and down. Outlined on the board in fat red bulbs was a cylinder with a rounded base and arrowlike dimpled head, from which came a cascade of white twinklelights. I said, they are going to put you in the pokey, young man.

"On what grounds?"

You've got a *dick* up there, Nils.

"Margaret! That's a phallus. It's a sacred symbol of the Old Religion. You should be proud."

Your religion is not my religion.

"It is but you won't see it," purred Nils.

At least he wasn't getting Bilbo in trouble anymore. And did Nils have a happy holiday. The Christian community was absolutely horrified by his anti-Christmas light show. They wrote letters to the *Press-Dispatch*, they screamed bloody murder on all the local radio talk shows, they snuck in twice and tore down his lights. The second time Nils caught them and called the cops, and when they refused to do anything Nils really went to town. He got more coverage in the *Press-Dispatch*, and some of the out-of-town papers picked up the story too. He made a big speech in front of city council, which was cablecast on public access

AR

TV. He made a tape of it and sent it to me. "Do you approve?" he wrote on it.

He even got a reaction from Dave Baumgardner. "That little son of a bitch better watch himself," Dave said. "Because *God*'s watching him, and God knows what he is."

I thought about it a lot. I watched the tape (I had already seen the whole thing live on cable) and then got my stationery and wrote Nils a very long letter. By that time I had learned that it was no good trying to talk to him; he would interrupt and argue me down in some clever way or say something cute to distract me. But if I gave him words on a page, he couldn't talk back, he'd have to pay attention.

First of all, I went into how I personally felt about the Satan game he was now playing. I had no idea whether he was still a practicing Wiccan or not; that was his business, but he had called himself a Witch in front of City Council, and that was a serious matter. It was very bad form for a Wiccan to expose Pagan beliefs to ridicule or disapprobation by using it as the basis of clownish political grandstanding, or just to draw attention to himself. Worse, by using the symbols and slogans of Satanism in that light display, he was associating himself, and by extension Wicca, with Satan worship, which was both outrageously false and terribly dangerous for the Wiccan community, and he ought to know better. He had been one of us; had we ever once done anything to him, treated him with anything but love and care and respect? Surely he owed us the same consideration.

But then I went on: Let's say you don't agree with that. Let's say you hate my guts and hate Wiccans entirely, and want to see us all lynched from the county courthouse flagpole (which was of course *not* entirely outside the realm of probability in this town). Consider it then from a simple perspective of justice. You say to the Council that you are defending your Constitutional freedoms. That's a fine argument, but what you're not considering is that every freedom also entails a responsibility, the responsible use of that freedom. You are not acting in a vacuum. Unless you're a total deviant psychopath, you have to consider other people.

I told him, I really don't object to Dave Baumgardner's Christmas lights. At least they're hidden off the main road, where nobody has to see them, where you have to make quite an effort, in fact, to see them. And actually there is nothing offensive at all to me in lights that celebrate Jesus, because I think Jesus himself was pretty wonderful; if more Christians actually did follow his teachings people would take them more seriously. Anyway, where Dave behaved objectionably was in his peabrained planning of the light exhibit and his refusal to admit his mistakes, not in the lights themselves.

But your exhibit is different, I told him. It's on a public street, right in everybody's faces. And the images you are presenting are ones that you know very well people will find personally assaultive. You can't tell me you don't know that a representation of a naked erect penis will make men feel nervous and exposed and women feel intimately threatened. Maybe you feel they shouldn't be, but they ARE. And don't you know that there are people in this town who really believe that there is a supernatural entity called Satan, who is out to do terrible things to them, and when you put "SATAN" on your lawn in big fat lights, you're scaring them? If you want to talk about magic, that is the cruelest, most drastic magical technique, to turn people's fears against them, to play on their primal terrors and make them feel hexed. How would you like someone to do that to you?

I finally finished the letter. It was about ten pages long and so thick with ink I could barely get it in the envelope. I knew I'd have to take it down to the post office to get it weighed for extra postage, which was all to the good.

The lobby of our main post office is open all night, and I love to go there. It's half-lit, creepy, with skulky-looking people crawling around, but still it feels safe because it's a government building with a back room full of military veterans, most of whom I would guess are still combat-ready. I weighed Nils's letter and bought the postage, and poked it through the "Local Mail" slot. Now it was in the hands of our mighty vets, who'd make sure it got to him, and that I couldn't take it back.

When I first met Murphy I was a little scared of him. I met him around the time I first came to town, when I transferred to the university in my sophomore year, and though I was open-minded enough at the time he was too weird even for me. He wasn't a student, in fact had never attended school there, which made you wonder why he was hanging around. He was about fifteen years older than the rest of us, and you could tell from the condition of his teeth and his personal hygiene habits that something very terrible had happened to him early in life, and he was never going to get over it. He ran around with a bummy old knit cap on, wearing corduroy jeans that were too tight for him, so that the waist rode down to his hips, showing his butt crack.

I met him through some friends of mine who were involved with the campus film society, where he was the projectionist. The other kids had made a sort of a pet of him, because he was so bizzare and interesting. Also, he took an interest in us, and since he was just as smart as we were, it was irresistible. I remember once telling him that we'd had a lesson in art history that day about Mondrian. "Ah, the patron saint of linoleum makers," said Murphy. One morning he found me crying because I'd had a fight with my mother, and he took me to the campus media center and played me some Bonzo Dog albums. There were just little ways he endeared himself to me, but still I always kept a certain space between us, just out of a young girl's reflex for self-preservation. I never got to know him really until years after, right after my divorce, when I was costume mistress for a community theater production a friend of ours was directing. It was *The Adding Machine*, and our friend had invited Murphy to play the dead man who murdered his mother, a very insightful piece of casting.

You know how when you do shows people like to go out after rehearsals for a drink. Only Murphy hated bars, so we had to go out to the Cadillac Diner. I became friends with a lot of people during *The Adding Machine*, but the only one who seemed to stick after the show was over was Murphy. He was working then as an engineer at the campus radio station and was always getting passes for concerts, and kept calling to ask if I'd go with him. I tried to put him off, but the more I talked to him the more funny and nice he seemed, and some of the concerts he offered me were quite tempting. I started going places with him, and soon I was spending a lot more time with him than I'd planned. He was on his best behavior, he seemed like a safe date and we really had a lot of fun together. So, as anyone has to do in order to be friends with a person like Murphy, I overlooked a lot of things, like his teeth and his table manners, and his general dirty-old-manness.

There are so many men like Murphy where I live. Not that they're all as bad as Murphy; he's an extreme example. Padraic is more like the normal strain of local bachelor. A lot of them, like Padraic, have nice jobs and even earn a good living, but they live in circumstances that would horrify most people. No regular meals, no housecleaning to speak of, no sex except what they can rustle up by themselves.

Tam tried to fix me up with one of them once. He was a friend of her husband's and she thought we'd have a lot in common: he loved movies, read a lot, saw a lot of plays (including some of the ones I'd done costuming for). She arranged for the three of us to meet at one of the local microbreweries for lunch. It was sort of fun because it wasn't like a blind date at all; I just listened to him and Tam gossip about everyone they knew who was cracking up or having affairs. It seemed to me he was clearly in love with Tam, which over the years has been quite usual for guys Tam has tried to fix me up with. Although Tam and I just had ice teas, this guy had three beers and then a couple of whiskies, which seemed strange because it was noon and we were just having hamburgers. Well, he was probably nervous.

Afterwards, he invited Tam and me to come see his house on the Old East Side. He seemed very proud of it, and should have been; it's one of the most beautiful neighborhoods in town, and very expensive. The house itself might have been very cute. But the weedy lawn and cracked sidewalk and peeling trim made it stand out in an uncomfortably ugly way. Though it's customary to let your Old East Side home look a little neglected, this was beyond the norm. We went in the entranceway, pushing past a recycling bin crammed full of wine bottles.

This man is depressed, I thought, looking around the dust-caked place. If it weren't so full of stuff you'd think it was abandoned. The walls were packed with videos and magazines and books (he had Madonna's

Sex, which he offered to lend me—though I'd never read it, I said no) and old bikes and acrylic neo-action paintings (which were his—they were quite good). There were roachy dishes and an uncleaned bread machine in the sink. The only things that didn't seem to be dusty or foul somehow were the kitchen table and chairs, which he'd inherited when his mother died.

He took us outside, and got deep into a discussion with Tam about the shingles on his roof, which needed to be redone—a lot of them were missing. I was staring at the grass, comparing its length and general condition to that of the grass in the neighbors' yards, and wondering if there was enough difference between them for the neighbors to have a right to complain about it, when I noticed that our host was wearing what looked like a new pair of jeans. Maybe he'd even bought them just for his meeting with us. They'd been too long for him, and so he'd hemmed them himself. He'd done it with staples. I saw them glint in the sunlight.

Here near the university is probably the only place they can live, these mateless men with staples in their pants. They're not tough enough to live out in the country with the Klansmen and pickup truckers, and they'd never last in the suburbs because they couldn't keep their lawns mowed.

Nobody bothers them here. They can keep their little apartments and houses full of their parents' old furniture, letting it get as dirty as they can stand, living on cookies and beer (or herbal tea, in Padraic's case). Nobody gets nosy about their way of life or tries to change it, unless some friend tries to fix them up with a date, which they don't mind; it's flattering, and whoever the date is, she'll eventually go away.

I think there is an element in this type of man that always has in the back of his mind that he has only to snap to, tweak that little thing that's been wrong all along and he'll be just like the other men, the lovers and lawn-mowers. Or more likely, he thinks he'll find that special woman who will take him in her slender young arms and make him normal. Only that woman keeps getting younger and more unreachably beautiful every year. Every man is told from little boyhood that there is, somewhere, at least one unimpeachably perfect woman waiting for him: so save yourself, don't get trapped, don't take second best, you've got plenty of time. They're accustomed to the idea that age has no meaning in a man's love life, that he'll be just as eligible at forty as he was at eighteen. The trouble is, many of these men look up after years and years of holding out for their angel girl, and realize that the only women giving them sexy looks anymore are on TV or in magazines. True, they see men their age, even older, with great-looking females hanging off them—but those men are either criminally accomplished seducers or glamorously rich.

So here they are, these hordes of men who find themselves selected out of the breeding pool, and can't comprehend what's happened. Nothing in their lives has prepared them for this violation of what they'd been told was the natural order of things, the male's right to mate, and woman's obligation to make herself available to him. Everybody else has a girl— where's *theirs*? It's a crime, a sin, this girl-less state of deprivation! Weren't they promised—aren't we all supposed to walk into the ark two by two in the end?

It was clear when I first met Murphy that he thought of me as a romantic target. But he was like that with all the women he knew, always trolling for that one female who with a kiss would release him from the nauseating spell he'd been under all these years. It was a little disorienting to be around this man, who was always declaring his passionate yearning for love, at the same time going to such extreme lengths to make himself gross and unacceptable to any woman. He would have been a completely normal-looking man if he just had his teeth fixed, and washed his hair, and wore pants that didn't show half his bottom. I knew plenty of men who weren't any more mentally stable than he was who were married or had plenty of girlfriends. I told him this. But part of Murphy's problem was he could not listen to reason. That terrible thing that had happened to him so long ago wasn't just an ugly memory. It was in his teeth, half-rotted away by the psych drugs he'd had to take; it was in the way he was forced to perform secret rituals, the strain of not being able to bear to have anyone suddenly touch him, even to give him a friendly pat. He could go twice a week to therapy for a million years, and really get to the root of that terrible thing that had been done to him as a helpless child, but what of it? He'd need another million years to work on the symptoms, the tics and obsessions and self-mutilations he'd worked out to protect himself from that bad thing, all those years ago. At this point, he'd worked out a mode of living: warped, unattractive, but it kept him going all right. His defenses successfully kept him from destroying himself, or anyone else. He'd built himself an airtight shelter of weirdness; it was a miserable fact that that structure shut out any woman from truly loving him as a man wants to be loved, but what could he do? Would a diver open the door of his shark cage, just because he was lonely and hoped someone would drop by?

Murphy was always asking my advice about what he could do to get someone to love him. That was his dream, he told me, to be able to wake up and know that there was one person in the world who was thinking only about him. Well, that's never happened to me, and I don't think it has to most people, I told him. But Murphy had his own ideas about love; he'd heard it often enough described in the songs he'd been listening to all his life. Leadbelly and Buddy Holly and Leonard Cohen, they all said the same thing. It was good to have a woman.

Padraic, on the other hand, never complained to me about lack of love. Considering he was constantly surrounded by adoring animals, I doubt he ever felt too deprived that way. He had a very active social life, and got to know a lot of people through his clinic; that's how I met him.

Padraic was much more the sort of person you would expect to be a Wiccan than I was. He had that whole-earthy look, he rode a bicycle and ate vegetarian. His vegan extremist friends were always trying to convince him he should give up his practice because he was supporting the pet industry. But he said he thought there was nothing wrong with people keeping domestic animals, because we are domestic animals ourselves.

Padraic was very well respected in town, and did a good business, but money wasn't foremost in his mind: he wouldn't declaw cats or remove dogs' voice boxes, for instance. "People who can't stand scratching cats or barking dogs should buy stuffed animals," he said. Actually, the one great passion in Padraic's life that I knew about was shih tzu dogs, which have beautiful soft voices.

Murphy knew that I was a Witch. There seemed no harm in it; he certainly wasn't prejudiced. He had the old hippie ethic of accepting whatever unusual behavior other people engaged in, as long as it didn't hurt anyone (again, a very Wiccan sentiment). Some of his best friends were quite wonderful people, and then others were pretty loathsome. I'm thinking particularly now of Jim Felch. Jim had been crawling around the margins of the local media-theater world for about thirty years. I knew who he was by reputation. In better days, before he'd used up his looks and the patience of all the available women in town, he used to be what Tam called an evil sex machine.

I actually met Jim that winter; he had just started doing a late-night talk show on Murphy's radio station, and Murphy introduced us. Jim said he'd heard so much about me, grabbed my hand and gave it a slobbery kiss, then made me take one of his business cards, which said

JIM FELCH
Air personality

Jim went along to dinner with Murphy and me. Although it was a pub where you usually just had a hamburger, he ordered swordfish and jumbo shrimp, along with a couple of pre-meal whiskies and several imported beers (Murphy and I weren't drinking; I usually don't, and Murphy can't because he's on antidepressants). Then, when the check came, he announced he was short on cash. Murphy obediently picked up the check. I would have called the manager over and said, here's your new dishwasher.

Murphy had apparently blabbed to Jim about my being a Wiccan Priestess. "Heyyy, think you could make me a love potion?" Jim said, sinking on his beer-rubbered elbows.

Why? I asked. Who would you want to use it on?

"I don't know. You." He sighed and sank further. "I don't know. What I need is a *sex* potion. Couldn't you just do a one-night-stand potion?"

Why not just go downtown and hire a pro?

"I can't afford it. I'm broke. Anyway . . . you don't know what a man wants. You don't want some woman you *know* is only going with you because she's getting paid. You want a woman who really wants to *do it*. I mean, there are hookers who really want to do it. I mean, really want to do it. I had hookers who did me for free. Of course, that was, ah, not here, that was in L.A. Women just aren't as open for sex here. I don't know, I guess it's the climate, freezes 'em up."

I asked what the woman he wanted would be like. "I'd liiiiiike . . . ." He sighed again, took a noisy pull on his pilsner glass. "I'd like a six-teen-year-old . . . with the mind of a twenty-five-year-old . . . only, no, then she wouldn't really be a sixteen-year-old. What I want is the general you-know, blonde hair, the pouty lips, not too overdeveloped—"

"Why not overdeveloped?" asked Murphy.

"You've been reading too many porn mags," Jim sneered. "Too much silicone. You should watch the videos. Much better women. Much *younger* women. Specially the amateur videos. And the ones with *Suzee Box*," slurping noises. "I'd like to actually show some of those to you," he said, staring at me suddenly, "just to show you what I mean. We should take her to X Marxx the Spot, Murphy. You ever been there?" he asked me.

No. "See that's the trouble," said Jim. "Women are so unadventurous. You think just because you go to a porno shop, you're going to get *raped*?"

Though I would never tell Jim or Murphy such a thing, considering what they were, this was exactly why I had never gone to a place like that. Of course I was curious; of course I would like to take a look at this fabulous male world of retail sex I was constantly hearing about. I doubt it would have anything to offer that would please me, but maybe it would help me understand some of the things that had happened to me and to some of my friends. When I was younger I thought you could find out about male sexuality simply by having sex with men, but for a long time now I'd suspected there was a whole other dimension to it that the ordinary woman could never even glimpse. By all reports this was a danger-ous place for women, which is why the smarter and luckier ones never went near it. There had been a couple of times I had been tempted to just go into X Marxx the Spot and have a look around. I had a right to, didn't

I? It was a public place like any other shop. No, it wasn't. Because what it sold was male dreams. And any man who saw me there might think I was a creature come to life out of one of the books or movies they sold in that shop, and he would come after me and do whatever mean, rotten thing he wanted to to me, and everyone would agree with him that I had it coming; my being there had been *the signal*. Of course, I wouldn't tell Jim that; then *he'd* maybe come after me, thinking I'd given him *the signal*. Men so easily slipped into fantasy. To them, nothing about a woman could be taken all that seriously, because anything about them was an element to be worked into a potential sex scenario. Like my being a Witch wasn't my religion; it was a way for Jim to get girls into bed for free. This offended me, naturally, but then again it made me feel rather full of myself, to think, for once they're not sizing me up for sex; they're sizing me up for what I can actually *do*. Also to think, yes, you think you could get a potion out of me, but you're not going to. I can protect all the girls in the world from you, ha! ha! You'll never get them now!

Isaac Bashevis Singer said that the act of sexual intercourse was always sacred; it just had to be by its very nature, and I have always believed this. There is something numinous in the union between two souls, whatever form it takes. I didn't stay with my husband as long as I did for his sake, and certainly not for mine; it was the marriage that mattered to me. Being divorced was horrible, physically painful. I really did feel like my body had been hacked in two. Wicca was enormously helpful in making me feel whole again.

Wiccans tend to be pretty heartfelt people, at least in the Gulo Coven, and that's partly why we never got into sex magicks. To use sex as a tool, either for paranormal manipulation or for your own selfish fun, is just so sinister it really belongs in the Satanist bag of tricks. Because what sort of person sees sexuality as something to use as a means to an end? As a way to throw power around? And what sort of ethics would set this as the norm for sexual behaviors of its adherents?

Sex magick proposes this chilly, cleancut model of sexuality as an electrical circuit, with the human race divided into universally inter-changeable prongs and sockets you slot together to get your nice strong current of power, which you then use to drive whatever supernatural machinery you wish to set into motion. But sexuality is so much more complicated than that. Our brains, which it's been pointed out are our most important sex organs, are so complex. After so many years of shame and silence, people are now openly denouncing the relatives, teachers, clergymen, and other adults who took sexual advantage of them as children. Just think of all the literally millions of people that's happened to, who will never see themselves as quite normal sexually because of it. Then think about all the traumatic things that happen between adults in so-called normal, consensual sexual relationships—people being beaten, betrayed, deliberately humiliated, impregnated and abandoned, infected with horrible diseases—and you wonder how there can be any coupling at all without fear and anger. And you are going to just brush past all that and say let's do a nice little clean clinical sex magick? I don't think so. I think you're going to open a big fat can of worms.

There are reasons why humankind has always tried so hard to control its sexual energies. Because they are so powerful, they're tremendously dangerous. Traditionally, the old wise ones, who are no longer driven by their own reproductive longings and can dispassionately contemplate the agonies of love and lust, have tried to protect the young ones from their more hazardous urges. Also, they've endeavored to stop the bad old ones from preying on the young ones too eager and innocent to know any better. This is so prudent, and so important. Because once you get a bad young one—and you should know how easy it is to make one of those—the whole village is in for hell.

Wicca is the only major Western religion in which women are the predominant celebrants. This isn't because Wiccans liked or thought more of women over the centuries than the others did, but because they have always had more respect for female power. Jews and Christians and Muslims, for instance, try to control the feminine potential by stigmatizing and repressing it or denying it exists. Wiccans cope with it by ritualizing it: they give the priestess or solitary Wiccan practitioner her head and let the female powers of creation and destruction take their course in her. There's nothing particularly feminist about it. The mastery of an experienced wise woman is beyond value to those who can use her; and if she gets out of control, well, anybody knows how to burn a Witch.

This is another difference between Wicca and Satanism. The three ages of woman—maiden, mother, and wise old crone—are by far the most powerful archetypes in the Wiccan world view, and though there are plenty of men in Wicca it really is a woman-centered religion. In contrast, Satanism, being an offshoot of Christianity, is notoriously male-centered, its rituals devised and carried out by men and reflecting the most extreme dominant-male posturings. The only notable female figure in Satanism, again as in Christianity, is the young maiden. Only instead of being a symbol of inviolable purity as the Christian Mary is, she is the Great Whore, born to be violated and debauched. It's a consumer image, without intrinsic meaning: just a body to be lusted after, procured, and used. Anton Szandor LaVey popularized the idea of using a live naked girl as an altar in his Black Masses, which tells you everything about what he thought of women. How would *you* like to be an altar? Crowley advocated the use of prostitutes in Satanic rites, but those were probably the only women he could get to reliably show up for them, once word got around what a sick pig he was.

The real selling point of the Black Mass is the implication that you're going to get an orgy at the end. Just how this is led up to or eventually accomplished seems to vary depending on who's involved and how demanding they are. I've heard of ones in which the naked girl on the slab is the whole show (imagine lying there with the crumbs and drool and candlewax falling on you). The suggestion here is that she may or may not be there to service the entire crowd if they're in the mood. I've heard of girls being brought in just for that purpose, having been given drugs first so they can't fight, the old frat-house trick. I've heard of full-scale group sex, which would of course require a quorum of female initiates or paid women, unless these were gay Satanists. Crowley describes a peepshow arrangement in which the male celebrant of the Mass does a ritual penetration of a symbolic High Priestess (again, a hired woman) behind a scrim. But I don't call that a sex magick, I call it a miracle, for a man to perform under that kind of pressure, unless he were an utter creep, which actually he would have to be.

91

AR

As I mentioned before, the Satanist creed, popularized by the famously wise, stable and reliable Aleister Crowley, is Do what thou wilt. This is the big lie of Satanism. What thou wilt indeed. No one can do what they wilt, outside the realm of pornography-level fantasy. But that wilting, despite all evidence of impossibility, creates a red hot perpetual core of anxiety and anguish in those who believe in it, that they really can do anything they can possibly desire, that they're missing something if they don't. That's really what's kept the suckers rolling through those black leather ibex-horned gates for centuries. And, of course, it's at the heart of all mass-market advertising, which is what makes Satanism so American, absolutely more so than any teachings of Christ.

I didn't call Nils for a while after I sent him the letter. I wanted to give him time to assimilate what I'd said and to cool off a little if it made him mad. Maybe he'd even decide never to speak to me again, though I hoped not. It just seemed to me so much to our benefit to be friends.

But I never heard from him. About three weeks after I wrote to him I called him. His housemates said he wasn't there anymore. I wrote him another letter but it came back marked return to sender, and not in his handwriting. So maybe he had moved. I called information, but he didn't have a new phone number, not one listed in his name.

But then wild young people like Nils are always disappearing in this town. They come to town, scamper around and go out of control, then suddenly evaporate. They go into drug rehab or the mental hospital, or go home to their parents, or straighten up and transfer to an out-of-state college.

I wondered how my Nilsy was doing. I missed the little guy, though I realized I was better off not being around him. In order to pursue Wicca with the dedication it deserved, I was going to have to get over my attraction to tilted people, the ones who laugh at life instead of feeling it. People like that are dangerous.

TWO

It was no wonder Ken had given Brenda Zang so many glowing year-end evaluations, despite her obvious insufficiencies. She was so much like him, at least in her management style. She claimed to be aware of everything we did, though she barely came out of her office except to tell you she'd lost another five pounds, or tear around in a frenzy looking for some document she'd lost that she claimed you'd never given her. Sharonne said Brenda told her she went through our desks after we'd gone home, and that's how she knew what work we did. But I never believed she stayed around that long after we left. Maybe she switched a few papers around in our in-baskets as she pulled on her coat at night, hoping we'd notice and get nervous.

Basically, you could take two approaches with Brenda. One was to quietly do your work and avoid her as much as possible, as I did. The other was to tell her loudly what a great job you were doing, and then do as little as you could get away with. This was what Hulga did. She was the one remaining employee Brenda had brought with her when she'd taken over Sharonne's department the previous year (the other two had respectively quit and requested a transfer). Hulga was a real smile-Jesus-loves-you-you-godless-germ type who was one of Ken's old God's Family chums. Brenda adored her.

Hulga at first seemed to treat me more or less normally. Gradually, though, I noticed a certain edge of malice about her. She'd make little nosy comments to me about my clothes, or things on my desk or what I was eating for lunch. She'd come and point out some mistake I'd supposedly made, and stare at me as if I were lying when I explained why it was really all right. Once some computer disks I was working on

AR

disappeared, and I had to retype everything that had been on them; later I found them in her desk.

I took the disks; I didn't say anything. I saw exactly how to play this. I had no intention of becoming another SMAT casualty. I would speak to Hulga when I had to, and be perfectly polite when I did, but otherwise ignore her. I knew my job, and did it perfectly well; she couldn't get me on incompetence and knew it. Her strategy, then, would be to goad me into a fight, and then she could get me on "unprofessional behavior"/ "inability to get along with coworkers." Too bad, she lost on that one too: getting along with strange and difficult people was *my claim to fame*. Ask anyone in my coven; ask anyone who knew my ex-husband. She'd have to come up with something better than *that*.

A couple of times I caught myself thinking, why is she being this way? what did I ever do to her? But I stopped myself, fast. I was starting to learn then, there is no *why* when it comes to human cruelty. Trying to make sense of it is just the quickest way to go crazy.

There are workplaces where they forbid dating among employees. They didn't have rules like that at SMAT, probably because the men who ran it wanted to keep their options open. Sharonne was always telling me about how Greg, one of the mail room guys, was always trying to get her to go out with him. I asked her if she wanted to. "Why would I? He's the company joke!" said Sharonne.

Apparently Greg had approached every SMAT sex goddess at one time or other, but all of them turned him down as beneath them. He was tall, stooped, sort of marionetty-looking, wore polyester pants, made practically no money, drove a tired-looking second-hand sedan, and was way too eager. Sharonne was always showing Hulga and me little notes and toys and candy bars he'd given her, the sort of things that get passed between desks in middle schools. She seemed strangely proud of them. It was months before she admitted to me that she was seeing Greg outside the office.

"He's nice enough, but he's always all over me," she said. "I get sick of it."

The most common request I get from people is for a love potion. I always say no, which usually makes them angry; they're embarrassed enough to have asked for it without having to suffer the additional discomfort of being turned down. I try to be pleasant and reason with them. Casting love spells is like picking wild mushrooms. Even the experts can make very grave mistakes. How do you know a spell is even working? How can you tell whether or not someone actually loves you? What I never actually say to them is: I don't want to give you that sort of power over another person.

After our dinner with Jim, Murphy started getting very excited about the idea of my being able to do a love magick for him. I thought it was a harmless idea he'd abandon if I didn't encourage him, like the time he tried to talk me into posing for nude photographs, but he was persistent, and got sulky when he saw I wasn't going to give it to him. I really ought to be more sympathetic and see his point of view, he told me. He was in pain and I was supposed to be his friend.

I said he knew very well there were conventional ways of getting girlfriends, and that's what he ought to use. But they don't work for me, he said. Well, can't you just get along without a woman? No, for a while he'd thought he could, but now more and more he felt he had to have one, even if just for a little while. "I just want to know there's not something wrong with me, like I'm some kind of monster," he said.

What I couldn't tell him was, of course you are, or rather: You've built a monster suit around yourself, the rotten teeth, the sour smell of unwashed hair, the fat bottom peeking out of the back of your pants, a complex of woman-repelling things you've grown so comfortable with that they've actually become a part of you. It would take such surgery to remove it all now that you'd probably never survive it.

Even if I'd been cruel enough to say it to him, he'd never have understood it. His fragile mental ecology had blocked out all possibility of self-examination; if he were able to see himself clearly, he probably wouldn't have been able to cope with it. He needed to fantasize that he was more or less a normal, presentable fellow, and all he needed was a little push—a little better timing, the right pickup line, maybe a drop of Wiccan aphrodisiac—to make his erotic dreams come true.

In a sense he wasn't much different from a lot of men. They hate the idea of having to specially groom and dress and preen themselves in order to attract a woman, the way women have to if they want a man. They want to be loved just as they are. I don't need to tell you this doesn't go both ways. Murphy told me very specifically what he wanted in a woman. She would have to be no older than twenty-nine, preferably about seven to ten years younger, in other words the age he felt himself to be as far as his experiences with women had gotten so far. His goal was to work back up to the rightful number of conquests that should have accrued to him as a man of fifty. And each woman must be of commensurate quality to the women he'd been denied all these years: chic, sophisticated, playful and carefree, and as sexy as all of the fantasy girls in *Hustler* and *Penthouse* and *Celebrity Sleuth* and the better porno tapes. If some of them just wanted to fool around, that was fine, but at least seven out of the twenty (that's how many he felt he was owed) ought to say they loved him and mean it. That meant they would live with him, cook and clean for him, and basically do everything he wanted them to do, without wanting him to marry them. Because that wouldn't be fair, I'm not ready to lose my freedom, Murphy said.

Half the problem, Murphy felt, was he'd been too nice to women all these years. What he'd always done in the past was to pick out a girl who appealed to him and pursue her. Sometimes she'd say yes and go to concerts and movies and to dinner with him, and he'd think he was getting somewhere. But then she'd say, you're such a good *friend*, and that would sting a little. But the woman would always be really sweet, and kiss him when greeting him or if he gave her a present, so he figured he might have a chance still. He certainly lobbied them hard enough, pretending to be harmless as a castrato, while, with apparent innocence, lending them a book with graphic sex scenes in it or inviting them to join him for an overnight out-of-town trip. A couple of the more adventurous ones actually went along with this last one, and one particular one of these (I met her once, and wouldn't put anything past her) agreed to sleep in the bed with him in the hotel, but with underwear on and not touching. (Well, some of us love a safe date more than others.)

Bedazzled by such continued intimacy, he'd break down and tell her how he felt. Of course, she'd very tenderly smile and firmly repeat, just a *friend*, Murphy. Often he'd find out she'd had a boyfriend all along, or worse, she'd pick one up along the way right in front of him. He suffered extremely every time this happened. Usually it wasn't even a great romantic love he felt for the woman—frequently, his pursuit of her involved more determination than inspiration. He might feel comfortable with her and think, I could settle for her. But the rejection in such a case would be just as hurtful. It wasn't because the loss was the same as if she had been fantastically sexy; it was the sheer insult of her not really being up to his standards, but rejecting him all the same.

Murphy wondered: was there ever another man who had this problem? He looked in books, both novels and self-help, and the only male sex problems he could find were concerned with sexual performance and the compulsive need for sex without love. But Murphy wasn't impotent or oversexed, and he was full of love. The problem was in touching and being touched. He had never liked to be touched, and had been dreading it for years, but in his loneliness had reassured himself he could withstand it in the right circumstance. He dreamed of that magic kiss that would set him free. Maybe only magic, or magical thinking, would bring it to him.

The idea of having sex was very important to him, though here was the thing. He didn't really like sex. When he'd first had it, it had just been sort of excruciating. For a while he'd wondered whether or not he should just find a woman who wouldn't want to make love, but then he'd decided against it. It wouldn't be fair to himself; even if he never did it, he at least wanted the *possibility* of it.

This had been his idea: since his woman friends wouldn't cooperate, he could use a sex surrogate to get back into having sex. Only even though he'd read a lot about them in magazines, he couldn't seem to track down any licensed sex therapists that would actually train you by doing it with you. Also, all the therapists he contacted said they only worked with couples, people who already had a sex partner to practice with. So Murphy thought he'd improvise his own self-help treatment using hookers. I asked him how he thought he could learn anything

AR

from a bought-sex transaction that would be transferrable to a real human relationship, but he wandered away from this.

What he'd done, finally, he told me, was to drive to Chicago. The sex trade was much more open there; they sold entire papers there full of ads for call girls. He'd had a girl sent up to his hotel room, but she had a dumpy body so they just talked for an hour and he sort of felt her up. Then after he was done with her, he realized he still had lots of money left, so he called another one. This one was much better, more in line with the image he had in mind: tight butt, thong bikini. He actually managed to do it with her. But the thing is, it hurt when he did it.

That's not normal, I told him, you'd better go to a doctor. He ignored that and just said how relieved he was now that he'd at least done it. But he was troubled by this feeling he had when he was finished doing it.

"I really . . . *hated* her," he said.

Sharonne had a very strange relationship with Brenda. It may be they recognized each other as similar types, which excited their sense of competition as well as a feeling of special empathy. Here Brenda had succeeded in getting what Sharonne was always saying she wanted: fancy car, rich love interest, microscopic butt. On the other hand, she was very strange-looking, while Sharonne, though getting a little old for her bar-hopping party-girl routine, was still reasonably attractive.

Since I was now part of Brenda's staff, I had to move to a cubicle next to her office. My desk was right up against Sharonne's now, with just a metal wall separating us. Sharonne seemed very happy to have me there. She was always shouting things at me over the wall, which bothered me because it seemed so inappropriate; it was a pretty quiet office, and everyone around us must have heard the things she said, which were often quite embarrassing. She especially liked to talk about sex, and what was more unnerving, make comments about Brenda: how horrible she looked, how much her hands were shaking that day, how weird and scatterbrained she was acting.

One of the vendors we worked with had sent over a basket of food at Christmas time. As soon as it was delivered, Brenda snuck out of her office, grabbed the basket and started taking the things she wanted; then realizing how this looked, she tried to make it right by holding up each piece of fruit or container of crackers or figs as she snatched it out and asking if anybody else wanted it. I didn't want anything, and Sharonne said she didn't either, so Brenda and Hulga took most of it.

After Brenda made off with her plunder, Sharonne started to snarl over the wall at me that Brenda had had no right to take anything out of that basket, that it was really hers, since she did most of the work that went to that vendor and was really the main contact with them, since Brenda hardly even knew what they did for us. She said it wasn't that she wanted the basket for herself, because she would have just set it out and had us each take whatever we wanted out of it, but it was the way Brenda had taken it over that infuriated her, that she had had no right.

Well, I said, I guess I see how you could feel that way, but just as I said it Brenda came running out of her office and stood there staring at me in a very disturbing way.

I tried to go on with my work as Brenda went back in her office and came out again with the basket. Standing next to Sharonne's desk, in a trembly fake-sweet sounding way, she went over every item she'd taken out of the basket, asking if Sharonne wanted it. Sharonne said no to everything, with a weird sort of smirk in her voice. This ritual completed, Brenda and the basket went back in her office.

Brenda went well out of her way to be especially courteous to Sharonne after that. But from that time on she either ignored me, or spoke to me in a brusque, sneering manner. Sharonne had apparently maneuvered me into witnessed something I shouldn't have seen or overheard, some reenactment of a family scene or favorite moment from sixth grade, and now to Brenda I was somehow taboo.

Well, I'll be damned, I thought.

My covenmates loved to talk about the sacredness of life. I think it was a coping mechanism of theirs, sort of a neurotic displacement. Whenever somebody at work had done something particularly brutal to them, or someone had betrayed or cheated them, or one of the local psychopaths started a new series of rape-murders, we would wind up our Friday evenings in the Cadillac Diner, arguing about whether or not Witches should have abortions, or support doctor-assisted suicide or capital punishment, or eat animals. Naturally, they assumed there was a definitive Wiccan way to resolve these questions. Well, there is and there isn't. In the Old Religion we have ethics, but no moral absolutes. A Witch must think for herself.

My covenmate Linda, the one who worked as a ward supervisor at the university hospital, was very much against abortion and euthanasia, because she thought birth and death were sacred states and we shouldn't interfere with them. I asked her if she would allow for mercy killing if the person were obviously suffering and there was no hope of recovery. "You never know that," she said. "Doctors can't tell. That person might be thinking, 'For God's sake let me live!' People say they want to die because they're testing to see if the world will still accept them. They don't want to hear you say, 'Yeah, go ahead, die.'"

My personal morality allows for such a thing as a just killing. If someone was about to torture or kill me, I'd absolutely kill him first if I got the chance. And my relatives have been told exactly what curse will be put on them if they ever dare put me on a respirator. Even Linda doesn't believe in that. "Do what thou wilt, an it harm no one" are especially valuable words to live by when you realize that "no one" includes yourself.

Laura, incidentally, was the last person I knew who'd seen Nils before he'd dropped out of sight, since he'd worked at the hospital with her. But then she'd stopped seeing him and heard that he'd been fired. She said she didn't know the whole story, just that he'd been nosing around in places where he wasn't supposed to be, and they'd caught him stealing something. What was it, some piece of hospital equipment, patients' purses? "No, something out of the biohazard bins," said Laura. "I don't know what. It was something gross."

When my mother died that winter, the shock was not in her dying but in my realizing that I was still alive. I guess because she was the one who had put me in the world, I had subconsciously assumed that this also implied that she alone had the power to keep me going on this earth. For about half an hour after learning she was dead, I was literally shaking with amazement that I was still here.

Once that was over, though, I got through it all pretty well. It was really the first test of my new faith, that being a Wiccan wasn't just a playful thing but could see me through those fundamental, sacred moments of transition in my life. The night I got the news I made a special rite for her spirit, to welcome it to its new state. I gave thanks that she had had a decent span of life, and in relatively good circumstances. I wished she could have been happier on this earth, but I hoped she'd found some kind of peace where she was now.

She was living up north when she died, in a little winterized cabin she'd retired to with her second husband, who'd died a few years before. Of course my brother and his wife were up there immediately to loot the place. I didn't care; I have my own furnishings and appliances and there was nothing there I really wanted. But my sister-in-law called before I left and demanded, very nastily, that I come prepared to get my mother's dog, "or else I'm just going to let it go in the woods," she said. They didn't want it; they had two big dogs that she said would just kill Mom's dog if they took it home.

This was just like her, to abandon a defenseless domesticated animal out there to freeze or be eaten by other animals. And it was still only a puppy, just five months old. I asked her why she didn't give it to the Humane Society. "I won't go in there. They treat you like scum," she said. "You take a stray dog in and they act like they don't believe you, like it's really your dog and you're dumping it."

As it happened, the pup was actually a fairly valuable piece of property itself, a purebred dog with an AKC registration. "But you could never sell it," my sister-in-law said. "It's too old."

I had to drive up for the funeral anyway, so I agreed to take possession of the dog and figure out what to do with it. Before I left town I called my ex-husband and made him take Joel and Casper. He whined

about it, since he lived in an apartment complex where he wasn't supposed to have cats, but I wasn't going to leave them alone, and I wasn't
going to pay to have them boarded either; *he* could do that if he wanted,
they were *his* cats.

My mother was in the habit of having a couple of dogs going all the
time, probably so if she lost one she'd have another one to console herself with. Apparently her old dog had died right after she'd gotten this
new one. She usually kept me updated as to the state of her dogs, but
she'd never mentioned this new one to me, and my sister-in-law said
they hadn't known about it either; this little black-and-white sort of
panda-cat had been pouncing around the house when they went in there,
and they'd found the papers for it later. The dog's name, according to the
AKC registration, was Princess Pang of Pu Pu. "Mom must have been
really cracking up near the end," said my brother.

My first thought when I saw her was, this must be a shih tzu. And
sure enough, the papers said she was. I felt a little sad that my mother
never told me, because right in my coven I had probably the best shih tzu
specialist in the state. Padraic had been an enthusiast way back when
they were still fairly rare dogs, and would be so excited when I told him
there was one in the family.

The only shih tzu I'd ever really gotten to know was Padraic's dog,
Dersu Uzala, who was an all-black male. The impression I got from
Dersu was that these dogs were macho, stout little bruisers. They actually are, the males, but shih tzu females like Pang are dainty and
ultrafeminine, with their long eyelashes and round little Betty Boop
faces. Of course, all of them are beautiful.

I remember my first sight of Pang. I had just come in and was sitting
on the carpet, as my relatives had taken all the chairs, and saw her totter-
ing out of the kitchen towards me, wagging her pluming tail. She came
up quietly, very close. Then she threw herself at me and dug her tongue
into my ear.

Pang was just a little young dog then. She weighed about the same as
Joel, only ten pounds. She was barely paper-trained, and not housebro-
ken at all, probably because my mother wouldn't have had the heart to
have made this little dog go out in the yard during that sixty-below

winter they'd been having up there. It was just as well, since Pang was going to have to stay in my apartment all day. I could deal with dog papers, after all those years of emptying two cat boxes.

She must have missed my mother, and I think I saw her a couple of times wandering around looking for her. I sat her down and explained to her that her old mom had gone away and wasn't going to be there any-more—not in the sense of feeding her or changing the papers on the floor, though, being a dog, she might still be seeing her occasionally—but I was going to take care of her now. She seemed to listen and consider what I said. From then on she stayed close by me, wherever I went, and during the two nights I spent at the cabin she slept in my mother's room with me, on the shelf at the bottom of the night table. I think she was on the bed a couple of times during the night, but she never stayed there. Maybe it's because I thrash around a lot, and she wasn't as tenacious as Joel and Casper, who would fight all night for the choicest spot on the bed and make you sleep around them.

We kept up the pattern after I brought her home. Pang would sleep on the floor by my bed on a folded-up shawl (she didn't like a lot of padding, as in pillows or quilts). But she kept tabs on how I slept, because when I had to get up in the night, she would get up too, and curl up by my feet while I used the bathroom or got a drink of water. She had probably learned from my mother the little kicks and tics a waking human being makes, because she would always be there just as I opened my eyes, to kiss me awake with her wide, cool tongue.

I took pictures of Pang; one of them was so cute I brought in to show around at work. Sharonne wanted to come over and meet Pang, so I invited her to stop by on Saturday morning. She came with Greg. He was, as she'd said, all over her. And Pang was absolutely thrilled to see them. She performed her special Aloha salutation for them, a sort of African dance of crouching leaps done while shaking her forehead against the floor, followed by lunges up to kiss them as they bent down to pet her pretty head, where I'd pinned a little grosgrain hair bow (her first top-knot was coming on thick and fast). I realized I was going to have to open up my social life some more; this little dog was going to want to see a lot of people.

One day early on in the time when she came to live with me, she was lying on her back, having me rub her stomach (one of her favorite pastimes), when I noticed a little thing on her lower abdomen, like a little pizzle. It was a shock. Pang was a male? This idea really upset me, I don't know why. Tam suggested it might be a prolapsed umbilical cord. I asked Padraic. "Oh, no, she's a girl," he said. "The AKC would have gotten that right!"

I decided I couldn't have the cats back. They might learn to coexist with Pang, but then I kept having a horrid vision of her getting her eye swiped by one of those needlelike Casper claws. This not only wasn't going to happen, it wasn't going to get a chance to happen. I called my ex-husband and left a message telling him the cats were his now, completely. I threw out the catboxes and did a thorough spring cleaning, so now little Pang had a home that was all hers.

But I worried about leaving her alone all day. The books said shih tzus didn't make good latchkey dogs; they needed company. Maybe the solution would be to get another puppy, but then leaving two young dogs to themselves for nine hours a day didn't sound good either. I finally worked out a deal with Padraic for day care for Pang. Four days a week, when Padraic was at the clinic, she could stay there and hang out in the reception area with Dersu. Padraic said it would be good for the old man to have a pretty young pup around.

After we founded the Gulo Coven, I realized how joyless my life had been before it. And after Pang came to live with me, I realized how lonely I had been.

Since I didn't have a yard to exercise her in, and my apartment wasn't quite big enough for all the ramming around she liked to do, I got in the habit of taking her out before I went to work for a short walk and then again after dinner for a long one. I let her go anywhere that interested her, around the complex to check the little messages the other dogs had left, around the stream that went past the front door or down the road by the golf course to investigate what was happening with the local wildlife. Sometimes we went on for a mile or more; sometimes we spent forty minutes without making it out of the parking lot, depending what she'd found to do there.

The people who lived in one of the houses around the corner from my apartment building owned a chow dog with beautiful brown-black fur like a bear. I don't know why but they never seemed to let this animal inside. They kept it staked out on their patio, and if it wanted to get out of the sun or rain or snow it had to go in a plastic igloo that was its only shelter. For a long time after I brought Pang home I deliberately avoided taking her out past that house. I wondered how strong that dog's chain was; I wished those people had built a fence. I had heard a sickening story once about a chow and a baby.

The first time we passed this chow Pang stopped, as she usually does when she sees another dog, and stared at him quietly. The chow stood and stared back. Then it sidestepped over to a shrub and very dramatically lifted its leg, letting out an impressive golden stream. Pang leapt straight up and scampered back towards our building. For weeks afterward she practiced going with her leg up.

Pang wasn't like any other dog I'd ever lived with. The others were all European breeds, and her ancestors had been bred in Asia, the descendants of Tibetan wolves. When she'd lie on her back on my lap, thrashing her legs around (this was her way of ordering me to rub her stomach), lolling her tongue and rolling her eyeballs, she looked just like the flying dragons in traditional Chinese art. Her hair wasn't wiry or silky or bristly like a Western dog's, but soft and fine and dense, almost cotton candy-like. She didn't have haunches exactly, like a usual dog's; when she sat, she just sat flat, with her little back legs sticking straight out.

The shih tzus have a very tragic history; they were politically persecuted animals. They were originally sacred dogs in Tibetan Buddhist temples, relatives of the lhasa apso and Tibetan terrier. They were given as gifts to very revered and noble people, which is how the Chinese ruling dynasty got them, and only these aristocrats could legally own them. The royal eunuchs bred them to look like little lions, which is why their name means "son of the lion." When the Communists took over in 1949, they ordered all of the royal dogs killed. But some English dog fanciers had managed to get a few out of the country before then, and Pang and all the other shih tzus alive today are descendants of these refugee dogs. Because the breeding pool was so small, the kennel clubs gave permission for them to be interbred with pekes and lhasas, so technically there is really no such thing as a purebred shih tzu. Pang has a definite lhasa snout.

I think about the holocaust of shih tzus, and then about the inquisition against witches, and what it means for Pang and me to live here together in this country where no one has a right to kill us just for who we are. It makes me feel very patriotic. And I think of the Chinese legend of the man who could ride his shih tzu through the sky, and it makes me want to take extra care of Pang and pay her every respect. Because if things should change, and we ever needed to escape, you never know, my dog could be my broom.

Some of the happiest days of Pang's life were when Tam would come over with Larkin and Amis. Larkin was about five when I first got Pang, and he had some concept of ingratiating himself with her; he would bring her rawhide bones and pet her and let her play with him. Amis was still a little cookie monster, so he mostly just screamed and lobbed little plastic dinosaurs at her. But Pang adored them both and would just follow them everywhere. Whenever they'd leave she'd make a little sound like, "Aww!" She was a little mother at heart.

Like all humans and dogs, Pang was a pack animal, and had to test me to see where she stood with me. I was never very authoritarian with her; it didn't make sense to me to drill her with the usual sit-stand-heel business, since I could just pick her up and put her down wherever I wanted her to be, and there was no risk of her knocking me over. When I compare the way the children I know are being raised now and the way people train their dogs, it flabbergasts me. On one hand total anarchy, on the other hand the most extreme bondage-and-discipline. I know people who nurse their children and keep them in diapers till they're practically ready for kindergarten, but will bang off the walls if their poor little dog soils the carpet. My philosophy is, you shouldn't have children or animals if you're afraid of a little poop. Anyway, once she came to live with me, Pang practically house-trained herself, as she's very fastidious and would rather take advantage of her walks to utilize this special means of communicating with all her dog friends. Still, I always keep a pad of newspapers on the floor in case she has to go to the bathroom on short notice. A dog should never be made to feel its natural functions are a "mistake." And how would *you* like to have to wait for someone to let you out every time you had to go?

I've never punished her, and the only time I ever really scolded her was so hard on both of us I never did it again. She loved to try to sneak out the door of our apartment and run down the hall, which of course I couldn't let her do and she knew it, but her favorite game was to try anyway whenever she could. I got very good at holding her in, but a few times she'd manage to get past me and prance around, dodging me when I tried to catch her. One day she actually got into somebody's apartment and it was crazy; it took me twenty minutes to corner her. Luckily the people thought it was pretty hilarious, and she didn't knock over anything important while she was tearing all over and under their furniture, but it wasn't the sort of thing you'd want happening again. I got her home and told her she'd better not do that again, I was very angry, I wasn't kidding and she'd better listen to me: what if those had been bad people who might have done something nasty to her? What if she had fallen down the stairs or somebody had tripped over her and hurt her, or grabbed her and ran away with her, so she'd never see me again?

Poor Pang took it to heart. She wasn't hang-dog, the way a European dog would be; I don't think it was even possible for her to hang that arrogantly uptilted head, or put that plumed tail between her legs. But she moved slowly, and lay with her chin pressed against the floor, and then curled up on the back of the couch and looked out the window for a long time. I went to her after a while and there were two tears caught in the corners of her eyes. I dried her face, and we kissed and forgave each other. It's better I don't have children! Just raising a dog is emotional enough.

One day I noticed there were little brown spots like tiny paw prints on the linoleum. I wiped Pang down, thinking maybe she had an upset stomach. But this wasn't Number Two. It was rust-colored, a very familiar color, and also a very familiar smell. I went to the dog books and they said a shih tzu could have its first estrus as early as six months. Pang was exactly six months old. How could I have been so stupid? I had put off having her fixed, thinking she was too young, and now the poor thing was in heat! I started having the worst burning cramps in sympathy with her.

But Pang herself didn't seem to be having any trouble at all. There was no pain in her eyes, though her behavior did change. She had been terrorizing me recently, biting my ankles mercilessly nearly every time I moved, as if to disable me so I wouldn't get away and would have to stay put and play with her constantly. But now the ankle-biting stopped. She stopped dodging around; now she floated serenely. The books said to keep her in or else all the male dogs in the neighborhood would be mobbing your house, so I stopped her walks temporarily. I also kept her home from her usual daycare and playdates. I was frightened at the idea of some animal raping my little dog.

There was a big bulging vulva now under her tail; where had it come from? I realized I couldn't go on cleaning up dog menses for ten days, so I went to the pet store and bought her a sanitary belt. It was a shocking thing to put on a little dog, a strap-on sort of G-string made of black vinyl that looked like dominatrix gear. Pang hated it, and became a Houdini at getting out of it. Finally I gave up on that and fixed her up with a pair of my panties, safety pins, and a maxi pad. She had no problem slipping this off either, but it was easier to get back on her, though not altogether easy. Pang had become very modest and indignant about being interfered with below the waist. On the other hand, whenever I did my sit-ups now, she would rush up to me, clasp my arm with her arms, and with a joyous smile tuck her little bottom rapidly in and out. It was adorable. I was beginning to think, when she's older, why not have Padraic find her a suitable mate? She'd have such pretty puppies, my little woman dog!

It just had to happen then that my ex-husband managed to wheedle me into taking Casper and Joel back for a week while he was out of town. I did it mainly because poor old Casper had what they suspected was feline leukemia. He had a bad staph infection, was losing weight, and they weren't expecting him to live very long. I put the cats in my bedroom and kept the door closed, but of course Pang, being so sociable, managed to get in there a few times.

Pang's estrus seemed to go on longer than it should have. It was supposed to last ten days, but well into the third week she was still wearing her panties. Padraic said it was probably normal, just to keep an eye on her. Then on Thursday night she fainted.

She was in one of her favorite spots, draped over the corner where the sofa arm connected with the sofa back, watching me in the kitchen. I came over to see her and was just preparing to pick her up when she sighed very loudly, and just slid down the cushions and lay flat on her side, rigid, her body tensed in a backwards arc, not moving for a minute. Afterwards she seemed all right, but was panting a little. I called Padraic immediately, and he said to bring her in the next day. I did, but he couldn't find anything wrong with her.

Her estrus was still going unsettlingly heavily on Saturday afternoon. I called Padraic's office—Padraic himself had gone camping—but they told me just to bring her in on Monday. It was hard to tell how she was feeling. She wagged her tail and ran and squeaked her toys, but that was just her personality. That night her bowels were loose and I noticed she had a dirty behind. I started to clean it up, but she struggled, and then she screamed, stiffening and curving her back like before, and fainted again.

I was scared. I took her to the emergency veterinary clinic, which was horribly expensive and certainly not as good as Padraic, but I didn't dare wait for Monday morning now. While the vet was examining her, she fainted again, right with the disk of the vet's stethoscope against her little bosom. The vet looked startled; she said Pang's heart had stopped. But then there seemed to be no trouble with it; when it did beat, it was strong and regular. Anyway, she suspected the main problem with Pang was a uterine infection, and so she wanted permission to admit her for overnight observation. She left me alone with a list of estimated costs for all the procedures what they might have to do to Pang, including putting her to sleep; I had to mark off what I was willing to pay for. I cried and authorized everything. So mote it be.

They let me call for progress reports through the night. Her heart was still strong, and there was no more fainting. They had her on an IV drip of antibiotics now. In the early morning, she had eaten a little and they had taken her for a little walk outside.

Around seven I went to get her. First I paid the bill, which ended up costing about two weeks' salary, about what I had expected. Then they sent me to the examination room to wait for her. I could hear her cry, probably as they pulled the IV catheter out. They brought her in, and I kissed her and she kissed me.

I took her straight to Padraic's office. Padraic looked her all over; he had a hard look at her bottom, then bent over close and took a good deep sniff. That was Padraic; with dogs, he thought like a dog. He said the best thing at this point would be a hysterectomy, but first we would have to wait until the infection calmed down. He gave me some antibiotic liquid to give her, and said to bring her in again in a week.

The treatment seemed to work; it narrowed her discharge down to a pink spatter, but the antibiotic made her dazed. I know how that works; they do that to me, too. She tottered around like a puppy, not knowing where she was, just letting go anywhere. But she was going to live! that is, if she would be strong enough to pull through the operation, which Padraic said was a worry, with her heart acting so funny.

But the operation turned out to be the easiest thing of all. Pang was the happiest hysterectomy patient there ever was; the day she came home, she bounced around in no apparent pain, paying no attention to the sutures in her belly. Within a month after Padraic finally tugged the little threads out, you couldn't see the cut anymore on her little pink stomach, where the soft white hairs were thatching in again. I could see now that the little pizzle thing that had worried me before was a vagina, obviously, exactly like my own, only with its pretty little cowrie-shell fold out in the open, not stuck away in a dark place like mine.

I thought of how happy Pang would have been with her pups and felt sad, but then this was the situation for both of us; we must find other ways to use our mother love. What I was really upset about was my ex-husband making me take Casper. Padraic hedged about it, but I was convinced that Pang got her infection from that diseased cat. Even though I'd divorced him, that man still managed to force disaster into my life, as always at no cost to himself. I had reached the terminal point with that rotten man and his guilt-trip cats. I wrote him a letter telling him I never wanted to see him or them again.

Poor little Pang lost three pounds while she was sick, which worried me since she was still a growing dog. I had always been very strict with myself about not giving her people food, but one evening I gave her a little chicken, and she just loved it, so from then on whenever I had something fairly plain, that a little carnivore like her might naturally eat, I would make up a little plate for her so she could have a couple of bites. It seemed to lift her spirits to try a little of what I was eating, and it wasn't that she was greedy, she was just interested in tasting it. I would never give her sugar or anything that would be unhealthy for her. And she, unlike most dogs I've known, would never just eat anything you gave her. She had a very well developed palate. She wouldn't touch vegetables, for instance, and the only fruit she liked was fresh mango, but it had to be dead ripe. Mangoes and steak were her greatest passions; they're my favorite foods too.

Pang's fur was what the books called changeling, a common thing in shih tzus. Her black fur could be the glossiest onyx black, usually when she was in the best, most lively moods, especially after she'd just gotten back from the groomer with a fresh shampoo and trim. Other times, when she was sleepy or a little run-down, it would be dull charcoal grey. Sometimes you could even see a little silver in it in the right light. Her white fur ranged from brilliant pure white to pale lemon yellow, depending on how much she needed a bath.

Because we spent so little time together, Pang gave our relationship her best efforts. She would always give me a big greeting when I came home, and stay close to me as I changed out of my work clothes and made supper. She would keep me company all evening, watch me get ready for bed and then tuck me in. Usually she slept in her bed on the floor next to mine, because my comforter was too squishy for her. But if I was restless or having a bad night she would come up and sleep in the crook of my knees. Though I think she slept through the night, she would always pay close attention to what stage of sleep I was in, and jump up to take a look at me if she heard my breathing get rougher or an eyelid flicker. Sometimes I thought she must be able to tell what stage of sleep cycle I was in, because it was always at the close of a REM session, when I had just emerged to the surface of consciousness, that she ran up to look at my face, and if she judged me to be sufficiently awake, kiss me on the eye or cheek. Sometimes she would stand on my head to show she knew I was awake, to stop faking now and get up. She knew when it was time for me to get up; usually, she was right within five to twenty minutes of my alarm clock. Sometimes when my need for sleep was desperate enough I would scold her or throw her out of the room, but that usually made me feel terrible. More often I would hold and ruffle her and sing her her special songs. We would have many great love scenes in the morning.

Having almost lost her, I now thought of our relationship in terms of the sad difference between her life span and mine, how I wasn't going to have her forever. I deliberately spent more time with her, took her with me when I went running or drove around on errands. Pang loved the car and had her own little safety belt rigged up in the back seat (the front passenger seat was too dangerous; besides, she loved to spread out). I also brought her along to Friday night meetings, which worked out fine, though I had to tether her to a tree in order to prevent uncontrolled kissing and ankle-biting during the rites.

She was a loving dog, but as she grew up her love bites could get a little ferocious. She shredded the hem of my cloak and my best pair of pants before I could persuade her she needed to be more nonviolent with us humans; we have delicate skins compared to a dog. Padraic said he'd never met a shih tzu with such a strong bite. He called her Jaws.

Sharonne was just terrible to Greg. The way she talked about him was amazingly nasty. "I figure if he's stupid enough to put up with it, he deserves it," she said cheerfully.

She wanted to be nicer to him, she said, but he got on her nerves because he wouldn't leave her alone. He kept asking her to marry him. And he was always over—hanging on her, cleaning her house, talking to her parents when they called her—it drove her crazy. And he kept coming over to talk to her at work, and even tried to kiss her, which really bugged her. I said she really should be careful about not carrying on at work. It could be a really miserable situation, especially if they decided to stop seeing each other. "You tell him that!" said Sharonne. "Maybe he'll listen to you!"

It was pretty obvious what Greg saw in Sharonne, why he tolerated behaviors in her that he wouldn't have in a woman like, say, me. She was a self-styled walking sex fantasy, just what he'd always wanted, and he seemed oblivious to everything else that went along with her. She never had a kind word to say about him. Obviously, she thought of him as a loser. "He makes less money than *we* do!" she sneered. On one hand, she admitted herself that she was basically just using him because she didn't have anyone else to go out with. On the other hand, she seemed furious and humiliated that she had been reduced to this.

One time Sharonne invited me and some people from work over to her apartment for a winter barbecue, and of course Greg was there, happily playing the man of the house, handing out drinks to everyone and supervising the grill out on the patio in his earmuffs and thermal mittens. I was thinking that maybe Sharonne was just telling me the worst about her relationship with her man, the way women always do, and that they might be able to settle down and just enjoy each other's company, instead of worrying about who was or wasn't fulfilling each other's wildest desires.

Then right after dinner Sharonne suddenly said something to Greg that just knocked the breath out of everybody, it was so mean and inappropriate. Greg said nothing. Sharonne smiled. Although we were all eating ice cream, I noticed Sharonne had a fresh bottle of beer in front of her. She seemed a little loud, a little tight around the mouth. The party had been going too well; she had to do something to break it up.

Pang and I were in the waiting room of Padraic's clinic one morning, waiting for our appointment with the woman who does Pang's hair, when Chris came out of one of the examination rooms with his pet ferret, Cognac. He looked thinner, tired and sort of stressed; I probably didn't look that great myself. "How you doing?" he asked.

Well, nobody's burned me at the stake yet, I said.

"You ever see Nils?"

I was just going to ask *you*.

The dog stylist came out and got Pang; she said she should be ready to pick up in about an hour and a half. Chris said there was a ferret-friendly coffeehouse nearby, so we went there.

"I kind of miss the coven," he said. I asked, are you still a Witch?

"No, I never really was. I only did it for Nils."

I asked when was the last time he'd seen him. "Not for a while," he said.

I said I hadn't seen him since Christmas, since the Christmas lights. "You're lucky," he said. "He's . . . it's not a good idea to be around him."

He took Cognac out of his carrier, scratched his little head and gave him some biscotti.

"No kidding," he said, smiling sadly, "you haven't seen him. I wouldn't have thought that. I thought he was setting you up for something."

You thought—

"Well, yeah, I mean, the way he acted around you, Mr. Cuddly, always climbing you like a jungle gym. I thought he'd probably moved in on you by now. Set up his little dissection lab in your kitchen."

Huh?

"I bet you didn't know about that. No, Laura wouldn't have told you."

Told me what?

"You know he got fired from the hospital."

Yes.

"Did you know why?"

No. Laura said she didn't know.

"She knew. She was the one who turned him in. At least Nils thinks she did."

AR

But that's weird, I said. Linda really likes Nils, and she's not a liar.

"I don't know," said Chris. "But Nils just thinks what he thinks, you know."

She said he got fired for stealing stuff.

"Yeah, and he was bringing it home, which is why I kicked him the hell out. I couldn't stand it."

What was he doing? What was he taking?

"Oh, that was the reason he took the job. He told me. He was in the perfect position. Running around in his little blue peejays, with his little cart, he could stash anything in there, they'd never know, they weren't going to stop him and *look* in there . . . he could just walk into any room, they never questioned him. If they missed anything, how would they know where it went? and most of the stuff he was interested in, they were *done* with, they did *not* want to see it again. Like this . . ." He sighed. "Like this big huge Tupperware I found in the refrigerator one morning. Ah. I opened it, there was this . . . ."

He covered his mouth, let out a whoosh of air.

"I think he must have got that one from the morgue," he said.

"But why he really took the job," he said, "what he really wanted, it was very specific, he wanted . . . . Well there's this thing, you know, they do in Britain, the British Witches, or Satanists, I don't know, this magic thing they make, that's supposed to make people dream. They call it the Hand of Glory. It's—"

I know what it is, I said.

I felt grateful now that I hadn't found Nils. The idea made me a little sick.

My god, I said, you should've reported him to somebody.

"I *did*, I turned him in. After I threw him out. I swear, I called the damn cops, they told me, you have to come down and file a report. So I went down, spent all day . . . nothing. *You* know. I guess . . . I guess that's why this is such a great town for sadists. Whatever you do, they just let it go, so long as what you're doing isn't stealing wallets or cars, or stealing Zootyfingers from Dave Baumgardner. If what you're doing, you're doing to *people* . . . I mean, regular, not rich people . . . Or if you're just *sick* . . . ."

He put Cognac back in his box, put him under the table.

"I knew a woman who grew up on the same street as John Michael Baines," he said, swallowing very hard. "She said when he was a kid he used to do things to animals . . . . One of her neighbors had a cat, and he caught it, he had a cat trap in his yard, and he cut off its legs, its back legs. And it lived, it dragged itself home with its little arms. And they called the cops, and they said why're you bothering us, it's just a cat."

What, you think Nils is a serial killer? I asked. (That's what John Michael Baines was.)

"No. He's not—*normal* enough for that. I mean to kill people . . . that would be too *straight* for him. He likes to *screw* with them more."

What do you mean?

"I don't know what I mean."

Then he said he had to take Cognac home, and left.

After we were married, when my husband got really deep into his true crime research, he started collecting memorabilia and wanting to decorate our apartment with it. At first I tried to have him keep it in his office, but as he ignored me more and more as the marriage went on, the things started creeping all over the walls. He loved the pulp detective fiction covers, and had a few framed reproductions, and as he got into *Rough Cuts* he started buying original crime movie posters from the fifties and sixties. I looked up one day and realized I was surrounded by screaming women and raised knife blades.

This wasn't as unsettling as what was in some of the books on his shelves, and even these weren't as bad as what was in the boxes in his office. Those were his original research files, and they had very detailed information about what some of the people he wrote about had done to other people, and photos of what they'd done. You think the movies and books that are out today are about as bad as they can possibly be, and then you look at what they couldn't even put in them and realize, we haven't gone as low as we can go yet. There's a big old crevasse down there still to crawl into.

One day I heard Sharonne snuffling and muttering to herself at her desk. Not that this was unusual, the muttering, but I'd never heard her cry before. Ordinarily I would have asked what was wrong, but I knew very well what it was and really didn't have any sympathy to offer her. Since I wasn't responding to her signals, she started making calls to people she knew—on work time, of course—and telling them, loudly and at length, how Greg had dumped her.

"I really screwed that one up," she laughed, sobbing. "He treated me better than any guy I'd ever gone out with." She told them how he cleaned her house, bought her things, and how good he was in bed. "He said he doesn't want anything to do with me anymore."

Later that day she called over the top of our partition to me to ask me if I knew any shrinks she could go to, because she was thinking of killing herself. Of course, now I had to go over and talk to her; you never just shrug off a threat like that. I asked, did she really feel that bad? She said yes, and this wasn't the first time; she'd actually tried doing it once before, but she'd cut her wrists the wrong way.

I said she should probably call her doctor, and do it now; forget about work, why not go home for the day, since it was obviously so painful for her to be here? "No, that's just what *he'd* like, for me to just disappear," she sniffed.

This was, effectively, the end of Sharonne's work life at SMAT. From then on, when I heard her on the phone, she was either saying something to Greg or about Greg. Whenever I had to go over to her desk to ask her about something related to work, she'd quickly switch off what was on her computer screen. She had something much more momentous on her mind than working now; she'd leave that to the natural burden-bearers, like me.

About a month after Greg broke off with Sharonne, she went on vacation with her family to visit some relatives in Arizona. She got back a week late because she'd gotten sick out there and had to go into the hospital. At first she told everybody she had had stomach problems. Later she told me she had had a miscarriage. She arranged a special meeting with Greg (who had been refusing to see her) to tell him she had lost his baby. "*That* made him feel like *shit*!" she smirked to me afterwards.

I am just not as frolicsome as I used to be. If I had become a Witch fifteen or even ten years earlier, the Gulo Coven would have been a much different animal. Very likely the rites we'd have done could never have been performed on public property.

I was very much a Goddess worshiper once, in my informal way. My body was a temple of ecstasy when I was very young, and I loved to dance, drink to intoxication and make lots of love. I would very happily strip down if the occasion called for it, just to be silly or seductive. It's lucky I've never become famous, I think, when I think of the pictures of me that may still exist.

I thought of my love and my pleasure as very much sacred things, but that got beaten out of me. Not by rape, though that happened; it's seldom a single blow that blunts us off, but more a process of wearing. Little bitternesses accumulated. The painful hours in gynecologists' stirrups being clamped open and swabbed, the sulfa pill-induced headaches, the slimy wads of antibiotic cream, the sleepless nights crouching in tears with a burning bladder. The demands for fidelity, housework, and constant availability; the parading before friends and family like a trophy of war; the progressive daily gauntlet of humiliations that were just-kiddings, what's-the-big-deals, just something you had to learn to put up with, to prove you were really in love. It was these invasions, starting so tenderly, but leaving me torn and stripped when the occupying forces withdrew, that really broke me of my sensuous ways.

Maybe this was the reason I spent so much time with Murphy then. I felt so much like him: warped, subterranean, fearing no one would love me, terrified that they might.

And here I was, a votary of the most deliciously erotic religion in the world. Does that make sense? You'd think I would have been wise enough to have slipped myself a little of my own sexual healing tea and let my body sing its loving song again. But insights seldom come in the easiest way, and I was going to have to face down the bad sex magick before I could contemplate the good again.

Padraic asked one night if we could do a rite of healing for Chris. Apparently he had been having some sort of mental problems, hallucinations and so on, and had tried to kill himself. He was under observation now at the university psychiatric hospital. I asked Padraic if he thought Chris needed anything, if he'd like me to stop by to visit. "No, no visitors," Padraic said. "They've got him in the locked ward."

Every time I came over to Sharonne's desk now, it seemed, she would be reading a piece of paper, which she'd put down quickly as she saw me, upside down with her hands spread over it. If I came to the printer while she was printing something out, she'd stand in a way that blocked my view of it and snatch the sheets out as they came, holding them flat against her body so I wouldn't see what was on them, as if I couldn't guess.

She told me herself she wrote letters to him. More than once she'd come back from lunch chuckling, and call over to me that she'd left a letter under his windshield wiper, "just to bug him!" I asked her once what she said in these letters. "Oh, just that I was sorry, that I wanted him back," she said.

About three months after Greg broke up with Sharonne, a friend of Greg's told me Greg had told her he had fifty-three letters from Sharonne.

Has he gone to the police? Has he told his boss? I asked. "No," said the friend, "he says he can handle it himself."

I told Brenda that it was really more than I could handle, doing Sharonne's work as well as my own, and Brenda said she'd look into it. What she did was leave early, and call in sick the next day. She never talked to Sharonne now, never went over to her desk. Maybe she went through it at night, but I wonder how that would tell her anything. Since the main body of Sharonne's work was now being left on Greg's windshield, there wasn't much left to check.

I was doing something by Greg's desk one day, and he came up to me and said, "Sharonne left a message on my machine at home saying she'd gotten engaged. Please tell me it's true."

I said it wasn't, that she'd told me she'd put her old engagement ring on her finger and was going to tell Greg it was from an old boyfriend of hers she used to fool around with sometimes before she took up with Greg. The object, of course, was to make him jealous.

"I'm thinking of changing my number," said Greg. "She calls me all the time, she leaves letters on my truck. I guess I shouldn't let it get to me."

I told him I thought he ought to let it get to him, that she had told me she had dreams about murdering him. "Oh, she won't do anything," he said. "She's just a whiny crybaby."

Sharonne was losing weight, she said, because she couldn't keep anything down anymore. This delighted her. She wore her tightest outfits and highest heels now, and even more makeup than usual. But I was noticing things had gone a little tilt with her. The heels were scuffed almost down to the metal, and there was a funny chemical smell about her. There were smears of something down the front of her favorite green dress; her blouses started missing buttons.

Brenda called Sharonne and me into her office one afternoon and was rattling on about the company picnic, which she was on the food committee for, when she suddenly went into this routine about Greg and his recipe for barbecued turkey. I just stopped breathing; I felt Sharonne go rigid next to me. Brenda went on about what Greg said that had cracked everybody up, about how funny he was, was he really always that funny?

"Ah, I wouldn't know, see, *Greg and I aren't together anymore*," Sharonne said, in a forced, fake-laughy voice.

"Oh, everybody loves Greg," Brenda blurted out, as if she hadn't heard what Sharonne just said. There I was in this room, trapped between two brains that weren't working.

I was taking Pang for her morning ramble one day, through a part of the neighborhood that we go through occasionally, but not that often. Pang had stopped at a tree by the curb, and was not really doing anything, just sort of sniffing and letting her mind wander, when a man bustled out of the house and stared at us. He was in shirtsleeves and a tie, a little fat man with a moustache, some sort of office manager type. He stared and said, in a high, angry voice, "Ma'am, could you not have your dog *piss* on my *lawn*."

The look that man gave me, the *rage* in his voice, was just so strange. I was angry and shocked—I mean, of all the stupid, rude, *unreasonable* things to say—but my impulse at the moment made me scoop up Pang and walk away, without making a sound. Just as if I had seen a chow dog standing leashless in his yard.

Humiliation overtook me quickly. I was so sick of giving bullies the right-of-way. But what would a man like that do to my little dog, if I had stayed to argue? I mean, I didn't know what he could do; he could scream at her, frighten her, run at her, trying to stomp her, come after her with a gun. A man whose sense of ego boundary was so fragile that the presence of a small dog on his lawn was an unbearable violation of his personhood might do anything.

As we went down the street, I saw him drive past us, in a shiny red mid-size car. My outrage had reached its peak. Here I was, a perfectly good neighbor to this man, here with my licensed, had-all-her-shots dog, walking here on a public sidewalk, with a little baggy of my dog's poop right in my hand (not many people around there even bothered to scoop, the way I did) . . . .

Well, it was too perfect. I doubled back; Pang hesitantly skittered behind, not knowing about this. Quickly, before anyone else came out to go to work, I raced to a stop in the middle of the fat little man's driveway, right where it intersected the sidewalk, and at the very central point shook my baggy out on it: a shapely little pile to greet this unneighborly lawn fascist. It was one of the simplest acts of retributive magic I've ever pulled off.

I was starting to avoid Sharonne, which was rather difficult to do. She would corner me and want to tell me the latest trick she'd thought of to annoy Greg, or to make him want her so badly he'd take her back. One minute she'd be telling me how she'd worn her extra-tight miniskirt or an old sweater of Greg's deliberately that day to tease him, and had already walked by his desk about twenty times to make sure he saw, and the next she'd be telling me about how she had fantasies of walking in one day with her husband's old semiautomatic and just blowing everybody away.

This was really scaring me. But I really didn't know what to do. Normally, I would have gone to my supervisor and said something. But my supervisor was *Brenda*.

Brenda had to have known what was going on. She couldn't have not known Greg had broken up with Sharonne—it was impossible that tidbit hadn't made it onto the SMAT chitchat network, with Sharonne howling and braying her grief and fury to everyone who didn't physically turn their backs on her and stick their fingers in their ears. Didn't she even notice that for literally months now none of the projects she'd put on Sharonne's desk had been touched, and that files that were usually on her hard drive had moved over to mine? If Brenda was so unaware, why was she acting so squirrelly lately, avoiding Sharonne like the plague, then suddenly coming out with that weird gabble about Greg and his turkey? It was probably part of some weird ongoing game, like the Christmas basket.

Who else could I go to? Santa? She would undoubtedly fire Sharonne immediately, and probably tell her I'd snitched on her too, and then Sharonne would come after *me* with her semiautomatic.

Besides, did I really have a right to interfere in this situation? It was Greg's responsibility to protect himself and to see that this personal problem of his wasn't affecting the rest of us. But Greg obviously didn't

123

see it that way. I began to realize he wasn't really uncomfortable about any of this. He was actually enjoying the attention. This was his revenge on Sharonne for disappointing him; it satisfied him to see her suffer and carry on. He probably cherished those letters. He had probably never had a letter from a woman before in his life, and by now he had probably upwards of eighty.

In my mind I tried to smooth out the warp of what was going on. Greg had said he loved Sharonne. But in my experience love isn't something that just evaporates if your loved one treats you badly. You still have some sense of caring for that person's well-being, of not wanting to see that person in pain. Even if he couldn't reason with Sharonne himself—and that was absolutely the last thing he ought to be doing, considering the scary way she was obsessing about him—he could have told his supervisor about the letters and calls and tight skirt parades, not to mention the murder fantasies. The obvious thing to do would be for somebody in management to arrange an intervention with Sharonne. They could have been very sympathetic, but explained that she must get help and resolve her feelings about Greg; they couldn't have her neglecting her work, and she couldn't go on harassing another employee. Wasn't this what Sharonne was asking for? Wasn't she basically screaming to everybody, look at me, I'm out of control, *stop me*? But now I could see that Greg and Brenda and everybody else were just going to go on pretending they didn't hear her, that none of this was happening, until Sharonne did something so weird or violent they would have to fire her. And then she might or might not come back to SMAT with her gun.

Sometimes we get confused; we find ourselves in situations that paralyze us, and we need to be taken by the hand and led to safety. I remember once when I was in college I was staying in a house where four cats also lived. One afternoon a neighbor's dog managed to get into our yard. I looked out and saw the poor thing trembling against the fence as all four cats advanced on him. They were posed in a sort of battle formation that covered all angles of possible escape, slowly moving forward in that way cats have while hunting, staring with cold, terrible looks at that dog. I ran out and tried to shoo him out of the yard, but he just curled up against me and wouldn't move. Finally I realized what he needed. I took the belt off my bathrobe and tied it to his collar, and then he let me walk him out.

Sharonne had worked for SMAT for seven years. For several months she had given Greg the use of her body and the social status that came from having a sexy girlfriend. Greg and SMAT might return the favor by doing something to help Sharonne regain her dignity, if not her sanity. And they might think about doing something for me, who had had to listen to her rants and mutterings and sobs and threats and cajole her and cover for her, just so *they* could pretend nothing was wrong.

It happened again. The lawn thing, I couldn't believe it. Again I was out walking Pang in the morning, this time on another street we went on just occasionally during our wide-ranging rambles. And again, Pang had paused beneath a tree, to contemplate nature in true Buddhist fashion.

We weren't even in front of this man's house, this man who came out of his garage and glared over at us. He was next door to where we were. The man was elderly, in his seventies, or maybe frail sixties. "I suppose you're going to come over here now and have your dog piss on my lawn!" he yelled.

Look, I said, it's no problem, I won't let her if you don't want her to.

It was like I hadn't said anything. He just shrieked: "I don't want your dog piss . . . it's bullshit . . . why don't you go piss on your own lawn . . . ." This was madness, senile dementia maybe, really frightening. I was seeing the sort of man who takes his old hunting gun to the neighbor's cat, who steers his Lincoln Continental into a crosswalk full of kindergartners. I picked up Pang and trotted out of that man's range. A couple minutes later, I looked back and saw him pulling out of his driveway— in a mid-size, late-model car, slick and red as a Doberman's erection.

What I really didn't get was the cars. Maybe it's a radio show, I thought. There were people on the radio at that time who had a lot of pull with men, conservative Christian types like Rush Limbaugh, who could tell his listeners to wear a dollar-sign tie clip or call feminists "feminazis," and they'd all do it with joy. Maybe Rush Limbaugh told them they should all drive red cars, and that dogs going on their lawns was an insult to their manhood, and so they were waiting in their garages

AR

now, ready to pounce out and scream all dogwalkers off the public streets, and run over them if need be, in their vehicles that wouldn't show the blood. Me and little Pang must have looked like such targets to those men.

I considered giving that old man the same treatment I'd given that other mean man. But I just didn't have the heart for it. There was not enough shit in my little dog to bury all the spiteful misery-makers in my world, and, really, I reasoned, why bother. Pang, as usual, set the right example for me. The very next time we went out, when we were halfway down the street, she paused and turned to me, crouched and widdled in the middle of the pavement. Having made this satirical statement, she then led me on our usual way, and did what the other dogs did.

The day after Sharonne told me that all she could think about was going over to Greg's desk and sticking a pair of scissors in his neck, I called in sick. When I came in the next day, they told me Sharonne had been out too. She'd called in and said she was in the hospital. This was wonderful news to me. I'd been hoping she'd finally break down and get some help. Then Sharonne's father called me and asked me if I knew where she was. I said I'd heard she was in the hospital. "Oh, yes, she was supposed to check in yesterday, but she ran away," the father said, in a nasty, snapping way. "You mean, you don't know where she is? You're supposed to be her *friend*. She didn't tell you?"

No.

"Did you know she was checking into rehab? She's an *alcoholic*, you know! Or didn't you *know*?"

No.

"Oh, yes, a quart of vodka a day. That's why she was in the hospital. She doesn't eat! That's why she's so thin! The doctor says she might *die* if she doesn't eat!"

Oh. I'm so sorry.

"I'm just surprised you didn't *know*. Didn't you notice something was *wrong*?"

I didn't want to say, I had no idea your daughter was alcoholic, I just thought she was psychotic. I said, it's terrible you have to go through this. I wish I could help but I just don't know where she is.

"Well, do you know somebody who *might* know."

Have you tried Greg, I said.

"Why would *Greg* know? Who's *Greg*?"

Sharonne tried coming to work one day, about three weeks after her disappearance. She said she had finally gone to the rehab clinic, and had been in treatment for eleven days, but I had never heard of an addiction program that got finished that quickly. She didn't look any different, just a little more tense. There was absolute silence at her desk all morning, till she asked me in a whiny little voice if I would go on break with her, so I did. I sat and listened to her talk about Greg for twenty minutes, until I interrupted and reminded her we had to go back to work. When we got back to our desks, I heard her call somebody, probably her recovery sponsor, to tell about how she had walked by Greg's desk twenty times that morning, but Greg wouldn't look at her. I got up and walked all the way around the building. When I came back to my desk, I could hear Sharonne telling her sponsor that nobody'd ever treated her better than Greg had and how great in bed he was. As afternoon break time approached, I took my work and went down to the first floor xerox room, where I knew she wouldn't look for me.

She didn't come to work for four days after that, and didn't bother to call in an excuse. The morning she finally did come in, Brenda fired her.

Greg stopped by my desk later that day, as soon as he heard. "Boy, you feel like the air's finally clear around here?" he asked, slapping me on the shoulder. I was unable to say any more to him after that, ever again.

That very afternoon of the day Sharonne was fired, a memo from Santa got sent around to everyone listing procedures for what to do if unauthorized personnel entered the building. Everyone who came in the door had to sign in and be given a name tag, and if they were not supposed to go in but did anyway the receptionist was supposed to get on the intercom and announce, "AN UNAUTHORIZED PERSON IS IN THE BUILDING. TAKE APPROPRIATE ACTION **NOW**." The appropriate actions were to call the police and take cover.

It is so strange to look back on, my whole time at SMAT. I remember one time, right after I started working there, when I was sitting in the break room reading and eating lunch, and Ken walked in and started gabbling at me. He naturally assumed that anything he had to say was more interesting than what I was reading. Anyway, then Hulga came in. They started talking about their kids, about disciplining them. Hulga said there were times when she just saw the devil in her little girl. She said there were times when she just had to grab her and shout, "I know you're there, Satan, get out of my child!"

Ken said he knew what she meant. There had been a woman in one of his prayer groups that had had something weird and witchy about her. She just interfered with the whole atmosphere of the group. Eventually they all became so uncomfortable they just had to ask her to leave.

I sat there listening to this, thinking, these people are living in the twentieth century. They went to college. They live in a town that has the highest percentage of PhDs in it in the entire Midwest. They work at SMAT, for god's sake. It felt very, very creepy, realizing these were the people I spent my days with. But I wasn't actually afraid. I wasn't thinking like a Witch yet.

They were always so cake-crazy at SMAT; any excuse to eat sweets was zealously observed. That's why it seemed a little eerie when my birthday came, and no cake materialized. Of course, cakes were supposed to be provided by the department that the birthday person was in, and my department was down to just Brenda and Hulga now.

One of the things I did get for my birthday that year was a collective gift from my coven, a gift certificate for an hour of floating at Child of Nature. I had always thought of float chambers as very unpleasant things that looked like big black dumpsters, like the one in *Altered States*, but Vivienne said those were just the old-fashioned test lab kind. The ones they had now were more like bathtubs, and you didn't even have to close the lid if you were claustrophobic.

I certainly needed to relax, and I hate to spurn a gift, so I went to Child of Nature. I was pleasantly surprised. They gave you a room all to yourself, with its own shower and dressing room, and let you choose what music you wanted piped in. I chose something as dreamy-sounding as possible. When I came to the float chamber I was completely reassured. It was a science-fictiony capsule shape of white plastic, with the lightest, most untomblike lid you could imagine, which you could leave open as wide as you liked.

I floated for half an hour, which was really no time at all. The most pleasant feeling of well-being came over me; I was altogether relaxed. I tested my body a little to see how it felt in motion, made it bob and sway in the warm, clear water.

To signal the last five minutes of the float session and prepare me to wrap up my business there, they piped in sounds of the ocean and the call of whales. And then I saw myself as a white whale swimming in the sea, with all my enemies coming after me with harpoons like Ahab, and me swimming free of them, faster and more agile than they could ever be. And this soothed me and made me even happier than before. I was singing as I showered off the salt water. I floated out of that chamber and swam back into the world, and felt ready.

One Sunday morning I was having brunch with Murphy, trying not to look as he snarfed down his runny eggs, when a rare bit of serendipity happened. Murphy said he had to return some videos by noon, but he wasn't sure I would want to go with him, because they had to go back to X Marxx the Spot. I said sure, I'll go, thinking I couldn't be more disgusted than I already was.

Since they had cleaned up the former skid row area downtown, X Marxx the Spot was the only retail pornography source in the whole county, a one-stop all-purpose vice outlet that had sex products in all genres, including a live strip show. I asked Murphy if he'd ever seen this show, and he said no, he wasn't interested in seeing the sort of women who would work in a place like that.

X Marxx the Spot was really a clever use of commercial space; it used to be a small 1920s movie palace. The auditorium part was where they had the live acts, and in the foyer they had racks of lingerie, magazines, sex apparatus, and a video section where Murphy started immediately poking around. I stood next to him scanning the merch. There were the amateur videos Jim Felch had mentioned; there was his favorite, Suzee Box. She looked like what a man Jim's age would think a high school cheerleader should look like. But Murphy didn't seem to go for the Suzee type. The women on the video covers he was looking at most closely were not the girlish type, but the sort of woman you think of when you visualize the word "whore": horse-featured with lots of makeup and feathery bleached hair, varnished-looking bodies with silicone breasts and those tight thong bikinis that made your coccyx cringe just to think of what they would be like to wear.

Near the counter, where a vast bruiser with a leather biker vest and Illustrated Man forearms sat calmly alert to the possibility that Murphy might erupt into some gross behavior that would have to be stopped, I noticed a bulletin board. It was covered with little cards, mostly for escorts and masseurs, with stacks of handbills and pamphlets on the floor underneath. One of them just caught my eye. I picked it up; it looked like it might be very dirty, threateningly so. It was black with red lettering:

Hey, man.
Want to
have any girl
you want?
Want to be rich?
Nothing makes a man feel richer than having a beautiful young girl by his side.
Want to be young?
Nothing will make you feel younger than waking up with a fresh, hot, gorgeous female next to you.
Want to be strong?
You'll never feel stronger than when you're inside a juicy young beauty.
Want to live forever?
Would you settle for feeling so good you know it'll never stop?
Want to get hot?
Go read your skin mags.
Want to get off?
Go buy yourself a damn massage.
Want to find the real, deep, inside-out satisfaction you've really wanted all your life?
Keep reading to the end. You'll get there.
Are you tired of hearing:

"No."

"You can't do that."

"You'll go to jail."

"It's wrong."

"You'll hurt her."

"You'll get in trouble."

"You'll get sick."

"You'll get killed."

"It's not safe."

"It's not healthy."

"It's not normal."

"You shouldn't."

You should. You will.

*Men, do you ever cringe when you hear the words "rape," "incest," "harassment," "sexual assault," "child abuse"? You should. These are **phony, anti-sex** concepts invented by **women** to make men feel guilty about their natural urges—and all too often, the deception works. We all know there is nothing normal about the way men's sexuality has been controlled, manipulated, and denied by women over the ages. Actually, it's **sick**. It's been scientifically proven, over and over again, that most of the problems that plague mankind, from impotence and depression to coronary disease and cancer, are traceable to sexual frustration. In other words, **if you don't get enough sex, you die**.*

*It's well known that females don't have anywhere near the sexual interest, intensity, or stamina of men. Therefore, putting women in charge of men's satisfaction is madness. The best argument against this sorry situation is that unlike women, men have a **natural, absolutely infallible** device built right into their bodies whose only purpose is to tell them whether or not it's right for them to have sex. **It's called an erection**.*

Let the erection make the selection.

Not God.

Not your mother.

Not the courts.

Not the politicians.

And not the women.

AR

What they've told you is fantasy is actually reality.

They just won't let you live it.

It doesn't matter how you live, what you own or what you look like.

If you don't have a cock, you're out of luck. If you've got one, we've got good news for you.

You don't have to pay for sex.

Not in any sense.

Never reach for your wallet again. Just your zipper.

Beautiful, young girls. Not on the other end of a phone. Not behind glass. Not holding out their hands for money. Not slipping you a restraining order or a paternity suit. Hassle-free. Disease-free. Hot. Wet. Willing.

Do we have to draw you a picture?

[There was a picture here.]

She's yours. Want to meet her?

Remember, it's free. Call 777-6666 for details.

It wasn't clear to me what was being offered here. Pornography? Prostitutes? a seminar for picking up women? a men's political rally? Maybe because it was so vague, it let you read it as what you wanted it to be. The picture on the back cover, the only illustration in the whole pamphlet, didn't look like advertising art at all, more like something the police would find in the collection of a seriously disturbed sex crime suspect. It was a photo taken through the window of a house, showing what looked like a very young girl, maybe even a child, pulling down a nightgown over her naked body. If it was staged, it was done by a genius, because there was nothing deliberately titillating in the scene: it was completely ordinary and natural, except for what was in the head of whoever was looking at the picture. Then I noticed, at the bottom of the back cover, the symbol, the upside-down star: the horned hunter.

"Hey, looks good to me," said Murphy, brushing by me to pick up one of the "Hey, man"s.

It was around this time that we lost our meeting place. How had they found out about us? The police might have been cruising by and saw our lights through the trees, though that was unlikely, or someone may have been snooping and reported us, though why such a morally upright citizen would be wandering around a golf course in the middle of the night was a good question. But what had we done, who had we hurt, to make them act so hatefully towards us?

They screamed at us, asked stupid and rude questions, shoved us up against trees, felt us up, bruised us, knocked over our altar and dug their fingers through all our belongings, hoping for drugs or eviscerated babies, I guess. It made them crazy not to find anything they could put us away for.

So to save their pride, they wrote me up for possessing an open alcoholic beverage in a public place (the chalice with the wine for our love feast). And my beautiful athame, the one Padraic gave me—they took it. I never saw it again.

Now we were in the papers; they called us a "witchcraft cult," and since I'd been the one that got the citation, they printed my name and where I lived. I felt angry and frightened, but comforted myself with the thought that at least this hadn't happened when I was working for Ken.

There seemed to be no repercussions at work, as far as my coven troubles went. The Monday after it happened, I found a broom on my desk. But that was it. No one did or said anything else, to my face.

One day Brenda didn't come to work, which wasn't so unusual, only she would usually manage to call in and tell somebody, who would then alert the rest of us with the merry news. But on this day we hadn't heard a thing until people started coming over to pump Hulga and me for gossip. Finally Santa told us the news: Brenda was in the hospital, in critical condition, with a ruptured esophagus.

People started talking about "when Brenda gets back," as though she was just out with the flu and might be coming in again by the end of the week. It was true, she probably would be back sooner rather than later, whatever shape she was in. And SMAT would keep propping her up till her head fell off.

I did wonder what would happen with my yearly evaluation. We usually got them at the end of the fiscal year so that they could give us our "merit raises" (really just cost-of-living adjustments) at the same time they were telling us how we didn't really deserve them. This year, though, because of the continuing repercussions from the Ken affair and our declining membership, they had postponed our evaluations for three months to save on the three months of extra money they would have otherwise paid us. It was true; they told us at a staff meeting.

All evaluations had to be authorized by Santa, who would automatically mark everyone down five points below the rating their supervisors had given them, besides routinely lowering all ratings she didn't agree with. The point scale was one to five, and everyone in the company was supposedly rated on a curve, although Santa refused to allow anyone to get a five. "No one's *excellent*," she said. "There's always room for improvement." The only people allowed to get a four were managers, who by definition were better than the rest of us. The managers got their evaluations first; Brenda had already had hers, so I knew Hulga and me were next.

It happened on a payday. Santa's administrative assistant usually walked around handing out everybody's checks. When she saw me she said, "Have you had your evaluation?" I said I hadn't. "Nobody gets checks till they get their evaluation." Apparently you weren't supposed to see how much money they had given you until it had been explained to you why you had or hadn't gotten your raise.

I didn't care about getting my check; I had direct deposit. And I usually didn't mind evaluations, because I'd just never had a problem with them. But this time my heart pounded. For a moment I thought if I hid under my desk they might miss me. But then Santa appeared as I was standing there in the hall, and gave me a look and crooked her finger at me.

"We're very disappointed in you," Santa had told me. "Very disappointed in you." I sat down at my desk with my evaluation form and looked at it but couldn't read it. Were all the things she said actually on there? I turned over a corner and peeked at the cumulative rating: 2.74. That was true then. Below average. I had done the work of two-and-a-half people, coped with madness and chaos, sweet-talked furious members into staying with us, smiled and said soothing things to everybody who came to my desk to freak out, and that was not average; that was beneath the standards of this organization.

Santa had blurred over the details of what I had done that so disappointed them. "Your work is *all right*, but it's not enough; you just haven't shown the sort of progress we would have expected. I realize you've been under a lot of strain with the turnover in your department and the shifts in workload, and you've actually done very well, but it's your *attitude*. People have complained about working with you." Who? "Oh, I'm not going to tell you."

I hadn't thought to close the door to Santa's office when I went in, and she hadn't bothered. Now I noticed Hulga at the door; Santa was smiling over my head at her. "Hey, Hulga, come in here," said Santa. "You can leave now, Sharonne, I mean Margaret."

They closed the door; I could hear them roaring hilariously as I escaped down the hall.

This meant no raise; it meant I would never be promoted now, or go anywhere at SMAT, except out the door, which is where they apparently hoped I would go before they would have to put me out themselves and pay me unemployment.

Santa had given me until Monday afternoon at five to sign the evaluation. If I signed it, they could use it as evidence against me if I ever filed a complaint against them on the grounds of, say, religious discrimination. If I didn't, I couldn't work there anymore.

Women who are being raped sometimes go into an altered state of consciousness, almost like an out-of-body experience, in order to psychologically survive what's being done to them. That might be why, as hard as I tried to look at that evaluation, I couldn't quite focus; I had to put it away. There was a shifting, unreal feeling; I felt as though my head and shoulders were slightly above their usual position. I looked down at my desk, at what needed to be worked on. I had just finished a big project, and all I had left to do was to file a few documents. I took care of that. Then I took down my picture of Pang, and took my hand lotion and spare sweater out of my drawer and put them in my knapsack, along with my evaluation form. I typed up a memo, printed it out and put in an interdepartmental envelope addressed to Personnel, along with my building keys, and put this in my out basket. It was almost lunchtime; I waited until I heard the first ding of the elevator, and then got my things and went down with the first group of premature lunchers, and never came back.

AR

Of course I had the usual thoughts about making waxen dolls of Santa and Brenda and sawing off their arms and legs, but then I thought no, the hell with this angry spell-casting. Think of the hate cakes; where did *that* get you?

Besides, I was learning, I wasn't the only Witch around. Brenda, Santa, Hulga, Ken. What hands had already made poppets of them, stabbed and burned and twisted them into the hideous shapes they were in?

I made up a new edition of my resume, checked the Sunday papers and the University job board, and started advertising myself. A friend of mine from my old job, the one I'd been downsized from before I had to go to SMAT, told me that since they'd let me go they'd started doing practically everything with outsourcing, and that if I was interested she could put me in touch with some people there who could offer me freelance work. I called her and got the names of a few contacts there, and sent them resumes. I also called the man who owns Under the Mask, a costume shop I've sometimes done work for, to let him know I was available if he needed my services. He was glad to hear from me; he'd been doing his pre-Halloween inventory and said his rental collection was in pretty pathetic shape.

Then, on Tuesday afternoon, someone called me from my old job and asked me if I wanted to take on a project for them; they'd give me two months to do it, though if I could finish it before then that would be great, and there would be more. I said sure, and a few days later they sent me a contract. It was a little disorienting. Even though I'd walked out on my job with absolutely no prospects, I wasn't ever really unemployed. I was more or less back where I'd started before I'd ever heard of SMAT.

I had to move. Until I found a steady job, I probably would have had trouble making the rent, and I'm not the sort of person who thrives under threat of eviction; but there was another reason. Because of that thing in the paper, people had started making crank calls and sending disgusting letters to me, and one night they spray-painted a building in my complex (the wrong one, but they did know my general whereabouts). I started asking around to see if anyone had a spare room to rent. It just so happened that a woman I knew from my community theater days who taught at the university was going away on sabbatical to Canada, and asked if I'd like to house sit for her. She said I could bring Pang, and she didn't even mind if we had our meetings on her property; we could even meet there before I officially moved in, as long as we let her and her husband watch. (They were pretty disappointed.)

It couldn't have been more perfect. The house was beautiful and huge, a Lloyd Wright style split level with a huge ground floor playroom that would be perfect for foul weather meetings. Even better was this vast property the place was on, all wooded around and practically invisible to any neighbor. If anyone intruded on us here, *we* could call the cops on *them*. (It also had an alarm system.)

Another nice thing about my new housesit was that it was so remote; anyone who tried to track me to it would have had a rough time. It had its own private drive, and the only way to get to it was by back roads that weren't even on most maps. Normally it was much more accessible, with a more or less direct route to the same road that went past my apartment. But that summer the township had started a massive road works project that would completely remodel that part of the main artery for nearly a full mile, all the way back past Zooty Farms. I assumed this was connected to last year's Christmas light disaster and the need to make the road wider. I really didn't mind; I love country roads.

One night I was driving home from our new meeting place, flipping through the radio channels, when I happened to land on Murphy's station. Jim Felch was on the air. I recognized his smeary laugh and old-radio-guy way of talking through his clenched teeth. He was taking calls, and someone on the phone was saying, "Don't you ever think, 'God, I'm gonna go to hell for this?'"

In response, over one of the studio microphones, there was a young man's laugh, very suave but natural-sounding. "Well, my response to that is, this *is* hell, nor are we out of it," the young voice said.

"That's an, ah, literary allusion," Jim sneered.

"Yes, well, the Devil is a big thing in literature, you'd be surprised," said Nils (that's who it was).

"Yeah, doesn't he in, ah, is it Dante's *Inferno*, where Satan gets all the best lines?"

AR

"I think that's Milton, Jim."

"Oh. Huh. *Well*."

"Anyway, I want to make it clear, I am not an intermediary of the Devil, I do not buy souls for Satan. I buy them for myself. And it's a good business. No money down, and the return is . . . well, how do you put value on a human soul? I don't know, I wouldn't want to be the one to do that."

"No, they're not like, ah, baseball cards or something."

"No, they're not like real estate, or art objects or anything. For one thing, there's no upkeep, there's no *storage costs*. And you never have to worry about theft. No insurance, that's another thing."

"Now how many souls do you have at this point?"

"About thirty."

"About thirty. Not much yet, huh."

"Well, I've only been doing this for . . . I guess four months."

"Four months, that's what, seven souls a month? That's not bad."

"Not bad. I got a big run on them last week, that brought my numbers up."

"Well, pretty good, *El Sin*. For those of you just joining us, we're talking to *El Sin*, a very enterprising young local entrepreneur who, you'll be amazed to hear, has *not* just opened up another drippy undergraduate faux-existentialist coffee bar or quote-unquote art gallery full of overpriced eyesores—"

"No, Jim, we've got enough of those in town . . . ."

"No, but this young gentleman is making his mark as sort of a trafficker in human souls, is that what you are, El Sin?"

"That's right, Jim."

"Now, tell me, *El*. You don't mind if I call you *El*, do you? Tell me, *El*, with all the blood-borne diseases around now, I'm thinking about AIDS of course, and that nasty strain of hepatitis going around, not to mention syphilis, and, uh, blood poisoning—"

"Blood poisoning, very bad."

"Yeah, ain't it. What I'm saying is, isn't there something a little queasy to you about handling other people's blood? I mean, it must get all over—your desk, and the pens you use, and—that's another question I wanted to ask, how do you, actually, get these signatures written? I'm looking at this big, black book here—I mean, these are nice, neat signatures, not like somebody took a bloody finger and rubbed it all over the page. How do you do this? Do you take a syringe and draw enough blood? Do you put in an inkwell, or do you use one of those old-fashioned fountain pens?"

"Good question. No, I don't have to draw blood, not like at the doctor's. You don't really need much blood."

"You don't."

"Well, it depends on how long your name is. But, no, you basically just, I have these little prickers, you can get them—"

"Little prickers."

"Yes. You can get them at any drugstore, any medical supply store, they're what diabetics use when they have to get a little blood sample, you know, to test their blood sugar. They can do it themselves, or I do it for them, you know, not a big deal. You just make a little prick—" Nils couldn't help laughing a little, as Jim was sniggering madly—"little prick, you know, on the tip of their finger, and you squeeze it a little—"

"Squeeze the little prick, mmm hmm—"

"Squeeze it till you get a little bead of blood, and that's all you really need, most people can sign a pretty good signature just from that little bit of blood."

"What kind of pen do you use?"

"I use a quill pen made from the feather of a crow."

"Mm hm. And is there any other thing they have to do to effect the transfer of the soul from them to you?"

"No, just getting the signature is pretty much it. As long as they understand that's what they're doing, and agree to it of their own will, that signature once it's on the page is a binding contract."

"And no money changes hands?"

"Well, what I offer them is not . . . things in themselves, it's not a material barter. What I give them is potential. If they don't use it, or don't use it wisely and get what they want out of it, what they think they're worth out of it, well, that's their lookout."

"As I recall, the original Faust didn't get a very good deal for trading in his soul."

AR

"Oh, no, Faust was an idiot. All he did was basically bop one girl, I don't know if that's worth going to hell for. When I go, I'm planning to have a far more impressive rap sheet than that."

"And so you will, I'm sure. Well, El Sin, this has been fascinating, I want to thank you for coming, or however else you reacted—"

"My pleasure, Jim."

"And after we pause for some of that wonderful stuff that pays the bills around here and what bills they are, we'll be talking to our favorite hometown spreadeagled-and-bodacious chanteusee Toni Michaels, a lovely lovely lady who'll be telling us all about her latest CD, so . . . ssssstay with us." A muddy-sounding snatch of jazz riff followed, and then a promo for the university personal crisis center. Realizing Nils wouldn't be on anymore, I turned the radio off. I had been sitting in my parking lot for nearly ten minutes, something that probably hadn't been very smart to do under the circumstances. Checking my pocket for my body alarm, getting out my car flashlight and shining it around to spy out any unfriendly lurkers, I made it up to my apartment.

I went to the phone and called the radio station. I asked for Nils. They didn't know who I meant. The little guy with the bangs, I said. Oh, him, he's gone, they said. I asked for Jim, but he was still on the air; they said they'd have him call me when he was through. He never did, of course.

I called Djanga. I had a feeling she'd still be up, weaving or playing her guitar or smoking cigarettes out on the porch. "No, you're not overreacting," she told me, when I asked her. "Being paranoid still doesn't mean they're not out to get you."

I suppose he has a right to do what he wants, I said.

"No. This is NOT about rights."

I heard the scritch of her lighter on the other end.

"I hate to say this," she said, around a cigarette, "but when you have Satanists in your neighborhood, it's like having a street gang. You can't reason with them. And you can't just ignore them and hope they'll behave. Especially once they start targeting *you*. Because if they think you won't do anything about it then they won't respect you, and they'll keep screwing and screwing with you till you say *basta*, enough, and give them back as much as they're willing to give you, so *check it out*. Are you listening to me, Margie?"

Yes, I said.

"I hope so," she said.

She whistled out smoke.

"I hope you're gonna pull yourself together," she said. "Stop acting like such a goddamn *Unitarian*."

I was starting to make the connection. I asked Murphy about that brochure we'd seen at X Marxx. He not only remembered it, he still had it. He'd kept it because he liked the picture on the back. I was so glad, because I wanted the phone number. I called from Murphy's phone. No one on the other end touched the call. It rang five times, then clicked to voice mail, where a digitized Nils murmured, "Are you ready? Good. Then leave your name . . . and your number . . . I'll call you."

I asked Murphy if he ever got curious about what "Hey, man" had to offer, if he'd ever called that number himself. "Yeah, but I was a little leery about leaving my number," said Murphy.

But that hadn't bothered you before, I said. What about your friend in Chicago? The one from the hotel: he had just told me recently that she'd called him to ask if he was planning to be in town again soon, because she'd like to see him again. You gave her your *number*? I said, shocked.

Sure, he'd told her his real name, where he lived. Because they really were friends. She didn't do what she did for all the reasons you usually hear, because she needed drugs or had been molested as a child; she just really liked sex, and figured that since she'd be doing it anyway she might as well get paid for it.

I said, that's just a line. Murphy disagreed: no, there *were* some women who actually did love sex, who *didn't* have any hangups about it, and if they were pretty enough they made a lot of money doing it. Actually, he had tried going to Chicago once after the first time. That had been the time he nearly got sideswiped by a truck on the expressway on the way there. He had figured that was a sign he ought to turn around and go back.

That night I called the "Hey, man," line, and left a simple message,

141

just Nils, call me, it's important and you know it is. He never did. I called that number so many times I started to feel like a stalker, but he never picked up the line. Always that mechanical voice.

I remembered a man who used to hang around town when I was an undergraduate. He was not a student but one of the older hangers-on, sort of an admired local character, especially among the druggy and punky kids; he used to pretend he was the reincarnation of Aleister Crowley, and stage black masses in people's dorm rooms and so on. Finally he admitted that he wasn't really Crowley, and everybody lost interest in him.

Well, that must be Nils' game, with the fairy-light cock and the book of blood: he was setting himself up to be the new fake mad magician on the block, the new Mr. Great Beast No. 666. But the way he was going about it unsettled me very much. Did he want to whip up a full-scale Satanic Panic? I had to confront him; I couldn't just let this go on.

If he wouldn't come to the phone, maybe I could try going to his house. I called the library and asked them to look up the number in the city directory. It wasn't in there, the librarian said; probably a new number. Maybe it wasn't even connected with an address; it could have been a cell phone.

This was pretty expensive, complicated mediaworks, for a little young unemployed hospital orderly. The first thing I thought was: He's dealing drugs. But wait a minute. That flyer, that girl on it; no, he was dealing something more complicated than that. Something worse.

Much as it sickened me, I called Jim Felch. This time he came to the phone; I could tell from his woozy attempts to be suave he would be receptive, and I might get somewhere.

He invited me over to come talk to him that night, after his show. That would be after three A.M.; I said even a Witch had trouble staying up that late. "Oh, I'll keep you up," said Jim.

There is nothing deader than our town, downtown, between the time when the bars close and the coffeehouses open at sunrise. It's absolutely terrifying, to see the streets so still and gray. You touch the sole of your foot to the pavement and it echoes like an anvil being flung in the street.

The radio station was eerie, half lit. I came in by the back door, left open for me. I was panicking myself with the idea that Jim was waiting for me in there alone. I had my hands in my pockets, clutching my body alarm in one, my carbon-steel kitchen athame in the other.

Of course there were other people there; both university radio stations have their studios there, the AM and the FM, and both of them are on 24 hours. Jim met me in the lobby, and took me back to the studio where he worked; there was an engineer on the other side of the glass digging into a boxful of wires, obviously with no intention of going home that night.

Jim was in a mellow mood. He had a bottle of blackberry schnapps, and urged me to share it, but I said I just couldn't. He offered me a cigarette; though I hadn't smoked in years, I took one, not wanting to seem stuck up. It was a Winston, simply disgusting.

So how did you get to meet Nils? I asked.

"Oh, he just dropped by the station one night with some dope," he grinned, Winston exhaust seeping through his teeth.

And you let him on your show?

"No, not that night, I invited him back."

To talk about his book?

"Yeah, well. That was what he wanted to talk about."

Did you know about his book?

"Yeah. I signed it."

Why?

He sucked on his filter, like taking a toke. "I thought I might not get another chance."

Did you do it before or after the show?

"After."

That's all it was, you signed the book?

"No, it was more than that, he . . . gave me some stuff . . . I went to a couple of meetings."

What kind of meetings?

"You know. Witchy ones."

AR

Well, what were they like?

"You know."

I held myself still for a moment, wanting so much to clout him on the head.

Think you could take me to one of those meetings? I asked.

"Oh, I don't think so."

Why not?

"You're too *old*."

At first I was flabbergasted. This man had at least fifteen years on me. Then the penny dropped. He meant, I was too old to be there as a *woman*.

So only young girls are allowed? I asked.

"*Yeah*."

So what happens with them?

"Oh, *you* know."

No, I don't.

"Well, I'm not gonna *tell* you."

It's secret, huh?

"Well, you're a *witch*, you oughta *know*."

But I'm not that kind of Witch, I said.

"Not that kind of *Witch*," he sniggered.

No, tell me, I said, what *do* you do?

"Well," he said, "you promise you won't tell."

I promise.

"You prrrromise?"

Oh absolutely.

"Okay, I'll show you," Jim said, pocketing his Export As. "I've got all the stuff back at my place. Come with me?"

I touched my athame, said yes.

My strategy was to hang around the inside door, claiming I had to go right away, so he'd bring it to me right there and I could get out quickly. But the minute we got in the door, he put his arm around my neck and put his tongue in my face. Oh no, no thank you, I said, twisting away.

"What's the matter? Don't you *like* men?"

I just stared at him, amazed. Now that was a question. Well, I said, I, I don't know, I . . . .

"Forget it," he said, "I'll get you the stuff."

It was the kind of felt bag you get with a certain brand of whiskey, royal purple, only it had been dipped in black fabric dye, and painted over the embroidered front insignia in red paint was the word *Faustling*. "That's what he called us, faustlings," Jim muttered.

Inside was a little medal, presumably to be worn on a chain, with the inverted pentagram insignia. This was supposed to be presented upon admission to the Black Mass, or whenever an audience was desired with Nils. There was also a little piece of tinfoil containing a clump of something that looked and smelt like old bong scrapings, with directions for dissolving it in wine for a love potion. Interestingly, there was no mention of whether the wine was to be given to the lover or the loved one. Also, a little plastic pot painted blue, full of what seemed to be strawberry lip gloss. This was a love balm that increased a man's stamina and endurance, and also enabled him to have multiple orgasms. (Oh, the devil is a liar.)

Then there was a little book. It looked handmade, bound in the same felt the bag was made from, only dyed with a reddish tint that made the purple a truly sickly, clotted blood-type color. The pages inside were printed with the same type, on the same red and orange-yellow paper as the "hey, man" brochure. It was titled *The El-Sinian Mysteries*.

"That's the manual, such as it is," said Jim.

Just glancing through it, I started understanding so many things. So much was clearer now. I breathed hard, trying not to let the tears come. I recognized a page here, a page there: something from a book I'd lent him about astral projection; there was a dream spell he'd asked me to copy out for him from my book of shadows. It was like death, to see he'd done this.

Did you ever use this, I asked.

"I *wish*. I tried a couple times, but I couldn't get it to work."

Get what to work, I almost asked, then stopped myself. Do you know anyone who did, I said.

"Well, some of the guys . . . Well, you know guys. They say they did, but . . . It's really all a scam."

AR

But it's free, right, I said.

Jim made a noise like a death rattle. "There's nothing *free* about it," he wheezed. "Have you seen what that guy *drives?*"

Is that why you quit? Because you realized Nils was scamming you?

"I didn't quit. I *can't*. The bastard's got my soul."

How do you mean?

"I mean, he*'s got my soul*."

You really believe that?

"Well, *somebody's* got it. *I* sure don't."

Moving to my new housesit was like going underground. Nobody knew where I was, how to reach me, except my friends and covenmates. For a while I was paranoid that someone might have found me out, might have tailed me to my new hideout. But my tormentors apparently weren't that thorough.

Now that I was feeling personally safer, I had a little more attention to give to my coven, which was naturally still feeling traumatized by what had happened to us. Something had to be done to restore our sense of solidarity and trust. I hated the idea of making them take an oath of loyalty; shades of another Witch hunt. But a code of confidentiality, by which a Witch could judge what would or would not constitute a betrayal of the coven or its members, would reassure us all. I introduced the Rite of Community at our very next meeting. A couple of people resisted, naturally, because what Witch likes to surrender even the tiniest freedom? But I had anticipated this and did not insist, knowing group psychology would do a better job of bringing them around than trying to throw some kind of tyrannical scare into them. In the end all of us joined in the rite. From then on we incorporated the Rite of Community into every celebration, to include every participant and onlooker. It was also then that I introduced the rope and the knife into all new initiations, and since them we have had no more hostile intrusions.

I had lost my home, my job, my sacred space. Naturally, I had some grieving to do, but it was a great relief to me at that time that I had my beautiful housesit house to spread out in, to wander through as I thought things out and laid my plans for what to do next. I paid no rent, and, since I had managed to pay off my debts while I was still working for SMAT, my expenses were practically nothing. I could actually live off what I was earning from my freelance work, and even put a little aside in case I would make enough that year to owe any taxes. Pang loved the house, and was absolutely thrilled to have me around all day. We took long walks, played fetch and chased each other down the enormous halls. She curled up at my feet while I worked, and made sure I got up and went to bed on a regular schedule so I wouldn't get lazy.

You would think after all the hair-raising things I'd been through— getting shaken down by the cops, getting run out of my job and home,

AR

watching fellow human beings crumble before my very eyes—I would have been prostrate with depression and anxiety. Not at all. Not for a long time, not since before I was married in fact, had I felt such energy, such excited anticipation of what the next day, the next hour would bring me. At times I was positively frisky, like Pang after a bath: zoom, zoom zoom. "Who lit *your* wick?" Tam asked.

It's true, even my coven meetings had taken a bacchanalian turn. Now that we didn't have to keep quiet, we could indulge more in music and singing, and because we no longer had the underlying worry of being discovered where we really weren't supposed to be, our rite-making became more leisurely; we took longer gearing up and winding down, and savored each moment to our total satisfaction. My covenmates seemed newly enthusiastic and creative, and came up with some wonderful new contributions: poems, songs, rituals. They even danced.

One night it was so damn hot, I decided to just forget my cloak and do the rites skyclad. I put on some Avon Skin-So-Soft, which I later heard is not really the bug repellent it's rumored to be, but it didn't matter that night; I came out with such a fierce attitude the mosquitos didn't dare touch me. "Oh my god, what have you been hiding all these years," Tim said to me.

Jude and Vivienne decided they wanted to be skyclad too. We ended up spending the first hour giggling and struggling to decide whether or not to remove clothing, and passing the Skin-So-Soft. We ended up all bare, except for Padraic, who kept his shorts on—he was still shy about his colostomy, but he'd get over it.

One evening after dinner Larkin called and asked, "Aunt Marget, can I come sleep with you tonight?" Then Tam came on. "How long's it been since you've had an offer like *that*?" she snarked.

I told her Larkin sounded sort of upset; was anything wrong? "Oh, yeah," said Tam, groaning a little. "Steve's out of town, and we're all going squirrelly here."

She told me that Larkin had had a nightmare the night before that had been so bad he wouldn't believe it wasn't real. The next day, he wouldn't let her open the windows, and made her keep the blinds shut and curtains pulled in every room. He wouldn't go in his own room at all, even in the daytime, not even to get his most necessary toys. That night he'd slept with her in her bed, refusing to sleep anywhere else. But then the next morning he said it had happened again, that he'd heard it outside the window and she'd slept right through it. That was why he wanted to come stay with me; he said I'd know how to protect him from whatever it was that was after him. I asked Tam, what do you think of that? and she said, "Look, I can't deal with him, he's scared the crap out of Amis too with this; could we just all come over and get calmed down a little?"

It was actually just what I needed, to get away from my own paranoid fulminations for a while and focus on somebody else. Tam and the kids came over carrying all kinds of pillows and blankets and stuffed platypuses and juice boxes. They looked very exhausted and strained, and seemed grateful for Pang's kisses and hula of welcome. I gave Tam a gin and tonic and the boys a couple of orange push-ups, and then I took Larkin aside and asked if he could tell me what the problem was.

He said he had seen this head outside the window, a flying woman's head with no body, just guts hanging down from her neck. That's awful, I said, and then I had to ask: Do you know why it was there, who made it come?

Larkin was astonished by this question, as well he might be. It had come there itself, to *get him*; what more could there be to it than that?

Well, it's true, I said, we don't always know why things like that come around. But you know it was probably a dream. "That doesn't *matter*," said Larkin.

I showed him a little room on the lower level, the bedroom of one of the house owner's older sons, that didn't have any windows, and asked if he thought he'd be safe in there. "Will you stay with me there?" Yes I would. In fact, we could all stay in there; I could move some of the furniture and tie up the ceiling swing and we'd probably fit.

Then Larkin came and held the bowl of salt water for me as I went around the outside of the house, making a protective circle that the head couldn't get through. "How long will it last?" Larkin asked. I didn't know, but I was sure it would take us through the night.

By this time the kids were more or less limp, so we tucked them into

149

AR

bed with Pang, and they conked right out. Tam had finished her gin, so
I took some wine and fruit and made sangria. I knew Tam was particularly sensitive on the subject of her children's mental health, so I avoided
mentioning the head. I put some soft jazz on the stereo and tried to steer
the conversation in a neutral direction.

At one point she said she was amazed, she'd never known Amis and
Larkin to go to bed with so little persuasion. Well, they're good
houseguests, I said, they're fine little gentlemen.

"Too bad they've got a crazy mother," she said, and started to sob. I
realized I hadn't seen her this drunk since college.

I've always paid close attention to my dreams, because I believe the
ones you remember have something to tell you. The dreams you remember are communications from your subconscious mind, so it's wise
to pay attention, though it's confusing sometimes. The subconscious is a
child within us, and sometimes its messages are as hard to make sense of
as the images in a very young child's drawings.

Have you ever had a hypnopompic dream? Those are the kinds
when you feel exactly as though you are awake, and have your eyes open
and are looking around you at the actual physical setting you are in, as
you lie in bed or wherever you are. The first dream I ever had like that
happened a long time ago, before I was married. It was summer and the
windows were open. I was lying on my back and could see and hear
everything in the room exactly as it was, the gray dawn light, and the
sound of what I'd assumed were some birds rattling around in the
eavestrough.

Then I heard a voice coming from just above the edge of the roof; it
was elegant, low and male, from a being I guessed must be about the size
of a person, or slightly bigger. "I was up here and I was just preparing to
feed," it said, "and I just had to tell you, I think you have the most *delight-
ful little human head.*" There was a chuckling laugh, and then it said
affectionately, "Ah, *je t'aime, je t'aime.*" I was terrified. I couldn't scream,
I couldn't move, as though I'd been injected with a paralyzing poison. I
just lay there in stress listening to that chuckle until the dream released
me, and then I lay in my gray room, eyes open now, trying to reason with
myself but not wanting to move yet until I was convinced there was

nothing on that roof, on the other side of that open window, that might react to my movements.

I've heard people dismiss dream interpretation by saying dreams are just a batch processing function of the brain, where data gathered during waking times are sorted out. That's a perfectly good model for how dreams happen, but a bad rationale for throwing dreams away. If you are neurotic, that means your present life is being soured by traumas of the past. So if dreams are just dealing with what's currently on your mind, those traumas will be a big part of the data included. You can use those dreams to identify those hurtful traumas, come to an understanding with them, and send them on their way.

Then again, this doesn't rule out paranormal influences, either. Tradition has it we are most receptive to psychic processes in our sleep, and also most vulnerable to outside forces. People who feel they are clairvoyant often have visions in dream states. Also, in legend, bedtime is when the night demons visit us, like the vampire and the incubus.

I didn't hear any more about the flying head after that night. Naturally, I never brought up the subject again with Tam or Larkin. Apparently he either forgot about it, or learned to manage his terror of it. But I kept thinking about it. It bothered me very much that a six-year-old would have an image like that in his head. It just seemed too sick and macabre to be a natural expression of anxiety. And Tam was usually careful about what books and television programs and so on the boys had access to, more so than most parents. There are plenty of people who think all horror and sci-fi films are fun and appropriate viewing for children, and maybe Larkin had seen something he couldn't handle at one of his friends' houses.

I ran into Bilbo, who had seen every monster movie ever made, and asked him what film he thought the gutty head came from. He said there was no such film. "That's too disgusting even for Hollywood," he said.

That night I was in the den working on an order I'd gotten from Under the Mask, for half a dozen opera capes. I was having trouble with one of the collars; I had made and unmade it so many times that it was beginning to be obvious I would have to throw it out and start over with new material. Still I kept on with that mad feeling you get when you know you're being ridiculous about something but are obsessively pushing yourself to do it anyway. Finally I realized I had stayed up too late; my brain had clicked off, and I wasn't going to get any more done that night. Pang was lying in the hallway, looking at me blearily like, please won't you come to bed?

I sat there at my sewing table feeling very funny. I had had an odd feeling all evening, like watching myself from outside, or as though a camera were filming me. In order to get to bed I would have to pass in front of a pair of french doors, and I suddenly didn't want to do that. I noticed how there was nothing covering the doors, no curtains or anything, and for some reason this suddenly seemed insanely dangerous to me. But sitting there at an angle where I might be seen through those doors, with nothing protecting me, was worse.

Finally I made myself get up; I ran across the room and into the hallway that led to the room I slept in. I left the light on in the den, though that felt like a bad idea. It might be interpreted as a signal, an invitation, but I wasn't going back in there. I went and drew the curtains, but then I wasn't happy about the gap left on the side at an angle where my bed would be visible from it, though I didn't want to get up and adjust it. I didn't turn off the lamp by my bed.

There was a rattling outside my window; it might have been birds. I fell asleep for a while. But then I was awake and aware of the window again; Pang was sitting up staring at it. I heard a thump on the glass and a woman's laugh, and then I wished I still had a mother to run to.

One night Linda called me, and obviously wanted very much to talk to me, but she could barely say anything for crying. She was usually a very solid, upbeat sort of person, so this worried me. I invited her over right away for coffee, got her settled down and asked what had happened to make her so upset. "It was a dream," she said, then, "No, it wasn't."

On the floor where Linda worked there was a lab tech named Eric Huang, who must have been very young, not much more than twenty. He was very cute, with black hair in poodle curls on top of his head, and he always wore silky black and silver and tawny pants and shirts, as though he was ready at any time to rip off his lab coat and go dancing. He wore a cologne that bit your nose, a scent like oranges, orchids and dope smoke, Linda told me.

Linda couldn't help ogling him a little, but tried not to be obvious about it; she wouldn't have dreamed of doing anything to make him uncomfortable. Anyway, as far as men went, she was perfectly happy with her boyfriend Jerry, who she'd lived with for twelve years. She just enjoyed having Eric there, and smelling him, and getting that teenage feeling around him. It seems she wasn't the only one. One day one of the nurses, a little older than her, about forty-five, was at her desk snarking off with her. Eric went by and the nurse said, "I don't know what *he* does around here all day 'cept walk around looking gorgeous."

Linda never worked directly with Eric, and so she never had a reason to seek him out. But he walked past her station about twelve times a day, and would smile and say hi usually. She would just be friendly, certainly never try to flirt. But he must have felt the way she was feeling. One day he tripped over a loose tile, and laughed like somebody who's being watched and knows it, and is completely embarrassed. Linda laughed herself and said she'd been waiting for someone to break their neck on that tile, and was he okay, just to put him at ease.

Sometimes they'd get off their shifts at the same time. He had a black van, and she would hear it as she walked by on the way to her car, sonically throbbing with the slow sex ballads they played on his favorite radio station. She'd think about the way those shimmering silks looked against his beautiful tawny skin, and once or twice, despite herself, she'd imagine the satin sheets he probably had (back at his parents' place, probably), and how happy he would look on them after she'd shown him what she could do.

Now this thing took place on a Friday morning, when it was still dark. She was in bed and Jerry had just gotten up to take a shower. She had woken up a little but had just figured out she could get away with another six minutes of sleep. Then she felt something warm on her left side, and smelled the smoke and scented fruit.

She can't remember seeing a thing. Just shapes, so close who could make them out? You know how it is when you're half asleep. And it was dark, the lights were off and the blinds were closed. She was on her side and felt this unmistakable feeling against her backside. She said she knew for sure it wasn't Jerry; she heard him in the next room. She wasn't afraid, it just felt very natural. She wasn't aware of hands touching her, or anything maneuvering her into the right position; she just snuggled down and it went in, just at her very favorite angle and curve of velocity. It felt so wonderful, it went on forever it seemed. But she had fallen asleep again when Jerry came back. He sat on the bed and was talking to her when she woke up. And she thought, it had to have been a dream. Well, it probably was, I said. "No, *listen*," said Linda intensely.

Who ever heard of a woman having a wet dream? She felt the evidence right on her, she checked herself, and the bedding beneath her; it was *there*, unmistakable. "You *know* when it's happened," Linda said. She was terrified Jerry would try to get back into bed, and the second he left the room she stripped the sheets and took them downstairs to the washing machine. She felt horrible, almost panicky, and the feeling didn't leave her; every time she thought about it she felt sick.

Three weeks later she had all the symptoms, but she knew she had to wait another three weeks to take the test. It was torture. On the day she did it, she made sure Eric wouldn't be on duty in the lab; that would have been too weird. The test came out positive. She was living in a nightmare now; she was terrified of telling Jerry; worst of all was Eric, looking so sad and puzzled now because she couldn't smile at him anymore.

It was probably a little slip you had with your birth control, I said. "Margaret, I don't *use* birth control. Jerry has a vasectomy." Well, I'd heard they could sometimes reverse themselves. "After *twenty years*?"

I had already decided I wasn't going to frighten her with what I was thinking. I made up another packet of sexual healing tea, which was unfortunately becoming my most popular remedy, and told her not to worry too much about what had happened. The thing now was to consider her situation and how she wanted to handle it. "I know how I want to handle it," she said. "I want it *out*, I want it *out of me right now*."

Well, think about it, I said. Be sure you're sure about what you want to do. Whatever you decide, I promise I'll help you through it. But, I said, I want you to get someone at the hospital or University Psychological Services to give you a reference to a good psychiatrist, an M.D., preferably a woman, and make an appointment and talk to her at least once, first, before doing anything else. "Do I have to?" Yes, you have to.

I was up with Linda until 5 AM, when she finally cried herself to sleep on my couch. I couldn't sleep myself. I was too weirded out. As soon as it was a decent hour I called Djanga. "Oh, *you*," she said when she heard my voice. "You know your friend Neil, with the Christmas lights?"

You mean Nils. "Yeah, well, he played a little *prank* out here last night. Hey, would you *mind*? Excuse me, my grandchildren are over." I waited while some sort of unintelligible rumble took place, followed by bright recorded music.

"I put them in the den to watch *My Neighbor Totoro*," she said, and I heard her lighter clicking, a whoosh of deeply-drunk smoke. "Okay," she said finally, satisfied, "now we can talk."

She told me what had happened. She had had a vague nightmare she couldn't remember very well, very hallucinatory and weird. The only thing she remembered was a naked man in a Dracula cape bending over her bed. She woke up feeling achy and dazed, and discovered that she was bleeding from the neck; there were two little pinpricks, like an imitation vampire bite.

Did you call the police, I asked.

"*Hah! Me* call the storm troopers."

But he must have broken into your house, to put those marks on you.

"Yeah, he broke in. Not any way *I* can figure out."

Or maybe it had been just a very intense dream, I said. And those neck things could have been psychosomatic eruptions, like stigmata.

I listened to the smoke circulate around her respiratory system for a minute.

"So what are we going to do about your friend, Margie?" she said finally. "He's a fucking succubus."

You mean *incubus*.

Silence.

"Oh, well," she said at last, ironically, "they're *reversible*."

Invisible mosquitoes crept over the skin of my arms. Then I told her

AR

everything: about Laura and Chris, about "Hey, man" and Jim's faustling kit, about Nils's little cottage industry, selling astral rape.

I heard a huff as she let go a long-held lungful of cigarette smoke.

"I think we should kill this guy," she said. "I'm absolutely serious. When you've got someone with that low a maturity level throwing that kind of power around . . . ."

Djanga, none of it's real, I said.

"So we're all dreaming this."

No, I know we're not.

She waited for me to figure out what I was trying to say.

Just because we can't figure out how he does it, I said, doesn't mean . . . .

"Yes it does,"said Djanga. "Smash him."

No, I said, *don't* smash him. He's not what you think, that's what he wants you to think. I know him. He's just a sick trickster, he's a manipulator, playing into everybody's fantasies, making us *think* he can do it.

"So he's sick. So you're gonna send him to the therapist, right, and they'll put him on Prozac and Zoloft and Paxil, and he'll have all kinds of recovered memories of what his dad and his uncle and the parish priest did to him. And meantime let him run around and play sicko games, and then what are you gonna do when he comes and fucks *you* in the night?"

I wasn't sure I was going to make it through this conversation. I put my head between my legs.

"I mean, he's obviously gunning for you," Djanga said. "Are you doing *anything* to protect yourself?"

I told her the formulae I had used up until then. "Well," she said, "I've never used that one. I guess it would have to work if it's kept him out of the house up to now. But, I mean, you do want to go out again, eventually?"

And what about you, I said, we've got to protect you too.

"You're damn right," she said, "I'm gonna clean that bastard's clock."

Look, I said, why don't I come over, we'll plot some strategies or something. "Yeah, or something," said Djanga.

I drove out to Maple Lake; Djanga met me with a big black candle and some piano wire. No, we're *not* going to kill him, I said.

"Why the hell *not*," said Djanga.

I started to cry.

"All right," said Djanga wearily. "We're civilized people here. We can work this out."

I sat in her kitchen and drank rose hip tea while she consulted her spellbook.

You think I'm weak, don't you, I said.

She smiled. "No," she said. "You've just never studied war, that's all."

She put down her book, and came and sat by me.

"You know, you're going to have to be the one to take him out," she said.

I couldn't, I said.

"Sure, you're the one to do it," she said. "Because you know the best way how."

I don't know what you mean, I said.

"Sure you do," she said. "You've got everything it takes. Just use your Witch brain and you'll see."

I felt this very uncanny feeling then.

"What I'm going to do now," she said, "is give you something you've needed all your life. It's a charm against bad men."

She went through all the steps with me, then had me do it myself, and gave me the whole double batch to take home with me; she said it would probably be more than enough to get me through what was coming. I should keep it in the refrigerator, and every night before bedtime, after I brushed my teeth, I was supposed to massage it into my teeth and gums for a full minute, and also into Pang's teeth and gums. "Of course you do her," said Djanga when I asked why, "she's your familiar, isn't she?" There was a chant that went with this preparation:

Evil to him that evil doeth.

Now what thou didst to me, thou'll rueth.

Try saying that while rubbing your gums with some kind of balsamic pesto.

I went to bed early. The next morning, I had to take Linda to the FemCare Clinic for her abortion. What a ghoulish gauntlet that

157

was. It took me and a volunteer from NOW fifteen minutes just to get Linda from the parking lot into the building a hundred feet away. I recognized some of God's Family, including Ken and Hulga, among the shrieking pack of demonstrators we had to force our way through. It wasn't entirely unpleasant, though. I had on my old hiking boots and I could tell from the reaction I was getting around me that the treads were still in very good condition.

It wasn't long after that that the man from Under the Mask called and asked if I could take on a special order for a costume. He would give me twice my usual fee, since it was an unusual design and might require a little more effort. He had the design ready for me; did I want to stop by and see it? I'll be there before you hang up the phone, I said.

I was glad I'd rushed. As I looked at the design I'd been given, a few salient points came to light. The very stance of the figure in the drawing, with his downcast head, upraised arms and clamped-together feet, suggested a feet-first five-pointed star, as did the outline of the man's goatee. The more I looked, the more other little tumbled-over pentagrams suggested themselves. It was like one of those drawings in a children's magazine where you look for the little hidden creatures in the drawing of a landscape, or the Hirschfeld cartoons, where you try to see the Ninas imbedded in them. It took me ten steady minutes of twisting it every which way, focusing and unfocusing my eyes, before, in that usual way optical illusions have, it jumped out with a boo at me: the signature *El Sin*.

I wouldn't even entertain coincidence. Of course he'd known I was a supplier to Under the Mask; of course he'd asked to have me do it. So what was the missing ingredient, the thing I wasn't intuiting? The nicest version was, he knew I wasn't making much money and wanted to be my anonymous benefactor. Second nicest: he just knew I made the very best robes.

Less nice than that: he thought it might be a kick to commission a robe from a White Witch, and then do something really disgusting while wearing it. Least nice of all: HE, my former disciple, was now trying to show me WHO WAS BOSS.

He had talent. It was a beautiful concept, this costume: scarlet lined with black, with winglike sleeves. It wasn't the usual Halloweeny vampire look; it would make a flattering, magisterial effect on anyone who wore it. This design would be a pleasure to execute.

I drove out to my favorite wholesale fabric outlet, a seventy-mile round trip, but it's always worth it. I found just the right thing, a shimmering purply red with a fine texture like miniature caviar, and some black to match. I made sure I'd have enough of the red to make myself a new gown for Samhain.

Then, it was time to gather my other materials.

I waited until after dark. I washed myself with antibacterial soap, anointed myself for good measure with some of the pesto Djanga had given me, and bedecked myself in all my amulets and my least best cloak. I got a flashlight, a plastic dry cleaning bag, a jam jar, a carton of salt, a bag of cotton balls, and a bottle of hydrogen peroxide; I put them all in my knapsack, and then I got in my car and drove down to the golf course. If the cops found me this time, they'd really have a story for the paper.

Maleficent magick rebounds, as I'd learned to my own cost. But then a spell cast under propitious circumstances by a well-informed wise woman will very seldom result in any harm, except where it is justly deserved. If the intention is clear, the mind is informed, and there is confident resolve, there can be no failure.

Before I began, I whispered into the water what my business was. I called to all my fellows in the water to join me in my purpose, if they willed it. That's why there was no physical revulsion involved, and why I could accept their sacrifice; we had made a bond together.

I never flinched. I said as I put my arm into the water: My friends, fellow creatures, I am taking you now as I will be taken someday. Nourish yourselves; you will nourish my spirit, and I will always remember you gratefully.

In one of the bathrooms in my housesit house, there was a ceramic tile counter full of plants, with a shaded purple grow light over it. I cleared away the plants and put the little creatures there on a towel to shrivel. The salt had played a part in their consecration, and now it would do its duty as a curing agent. They were young, slender, almost delicate; when dried and sewn into those eccentric, pointy hems, they were almost undetectable.

159

ANNE SHARP

Now came the final part of the costume, to cap it all off. The man in the drawing was wearing what looked like a pair of ibex horns. Of course this was the common Satanic image, but you might imagine how hard it would be to actually carry off this effect in real life. Real horn is damn heavy, and the human skull is certainly not meant to carry that kind of weight. I remember a fantasy headdress I had created for a production of *Midsummer Night's Dream* that used a pair of real deer's antlers. It was useless, because whoever tried to wear it for more than a couple of seconds ended up in tears. You could either go the realistic route and cast the horns in hollow plastic, or go for a more impressionistic effect. Given the look of the robe they went with, I opted for trickery.

I found a beautiful raw silk at Minnesota Fabrics that made the perfect covering for a soft sculpture of ibex antlers. I carved the foundation out of hard foam, which wouldn't wobble, and attached it to a wide velvet band that I knew would match Nils' hair exactly. Before attaching the horns with superglue, I slipped one of my little friends into a hollow I'd made in the base of one of them. The result, all together, looked fiercely impressive and was surprisingly sturdy. He wouldn't be able to resist these. I could see him slipping them on, staring at himself in the long mirror in the costume room at Under the Mask, slowly raising his arms to see the dazzling scarlet spread on either side of him like waves of fresh blood—

In a way this was worse than killing him. Was there anything worse you could do to a man than what I was about to do to him? I suppose you could kill him, but I think any man you'd ask would say that's what he'd rather you do.

And it wasn't even only that. I was doing him a double dirty. This wasn't like the hate cake hex, not at all, where you could rationalize it was for his good as well as everybody else's. This was an utterly, utterly destructive thing. Nils loved his work. It was really the only thing he could do on this earth, given the state of his poor sick soul, and I was taking even that away. No more faustlings, no more plush car—all his borrowed glamor stripped away, not to mention the charisma he was born with, the only possession he ever really had.

But this was what I had to do. I had to do it for my community, for

160

their protection. Forensic magick—he'd given me the idea, after all. And thinking over what he'd done, I had to admit it was fitting that he be my first test case.

I walked right into him. It was twilight, and I was coming out of the toy store on Main Street. He came at me as though he'd been waiting in the doorway. He was wearing a charcoal gray silk suit, a red boucle tie, and he had a very nice haircut. As he hugged me, I noticed he was wearing Fahrenheit cologne; I'd bought him a little bottle for Christmas. I hoped it masked the smell of adrenalin, that must be coming from me.

"You're a hard woman to get hold of!" he said. "When did you move?"

After you ratted me out to the Keystone Kops, I said.

He laughed and asked me if I'd eaten dinner yet. "I'll take you to the Atelier," he said.

I'm not really dressed for that, I said.

"Well," said Nils, looking me up and down, "let's stop in at the raw bar, anyway." He ordered us champagne—the oldest, Frenchest vintage they had on the list—and oysters. "High Priestesship looks *good* on you," he said. "I knew it would."

So tell me about the faustlings, I said.

"I don't know what you mean," he said sweetly.

I was just wondering, you know, what you do with all those souls you bought.

"Margaret, no, I'm sorry, I won't talk shop tonight. I'm too glad to see you. It's been like years and years and years. God I've missed you."

I've missed you too.

"Really?" he said, stroking me a little under the railing.

Why have you been hiding?

"I keep a low profile. It's good for business."

Have you been to see Chris, I said.

He chuckled. "In his *dreams*," he murmured.

That champagne was wonderful. I needed it.

"So!" he said. "Show me what you bought."

I showed him. It was a stuffed puffin.

"Oh, cute! Who's it for?"

It's for Larkin.

"You mean that little spew survived to see another birthday?"

You know, I said, I really like Larkin a lot.

"That's because you don't have any kids of your own."

He put his hand over mine.

"I always thought we'd have had the prettiest babies," he said.

He reached for an oyster, downed it with the ease of someone who's accustomed himself to swallowing strange things.

"Come on, now," he said, "you haven't had one yet."

I don't like them, I said.

"No. You never did like aquatic invertebrates."

He gazed into my eyes.

"I feel like being cozy tonight," he said. "You want to just go home and order a pizza?"

Sure, where are you staying? I asked.

"I thought we'd go to *your* home."

I shook my head.

"All right," he said with a patient smile, and motioned for the waiter.

He paid the check with the crispest, most pristine pair of fifty dollar bills I've ever seen, then gently tucked my hand into the crook of his arm and walked me to the municipal structure where his car was parked. I don't know cars; I don't know which make it was, but it had the strange contours of a European car, it was black and inside it felt like down pillows covered in velvet. I noticed there was a big Under the Mask box in the back seat. Suddenly I realized that what I'd been feeling all that last hour wasn't what I'd thought it was: I wasn't afraid. I was just horribly, devilishly excited.

Nils looked at me warmly. He was giving me that look that said, the talking part of this evening is over. He felt my heart, laughed at how hard it was going. What a monster he was, my beautiful monster.

"Take me home," he murmured. But I wouldn't.

We couldn't stay in the parking structure, there were people coming, so he took me down by the river. But it was a beautiful evening, and there were children, bicyclers, walkers, fishers everywhere. Why don't we go to your house, I said.

He drove me to the University Inn, gave the car to the valet parker, checked us in, kept his hand on the back of my neck as we rode up in the elevator with some snickering college girls who were about to sneak into the hotel pool, led me quickly down the hall, slipped the key-card into the slot of 333. Should be 666, I said. "This is as high as it goes," he said, locking the locks behind us. Then he came at me with bruising velocity.

It was a weird, breathless situation, wanting the magick I'd tailored to his adorable body to work, but then, my god, I'll admit it, desperately wanting it not to. Was it the firm determination I'd used in my spell-casting, was it the stale clammy whoosh coming from that horrid rattling old air conditioning system in that room, or did he not really love me after all? I'll never know. It was fascinating anyway, just lying there curled around the pizza box, looking and looking at my beautiful Nils, so uncharacteristically tender and soft, so obviously astonished. This had never happened to him before.

Despite what was so clearly going on, he seemed determined not to break character, to relax his mastery of me. Hoping I wouldn't notice perhaps, he gently decelerated his attack into milder caresses, as though he had just been teasing, and now had some more complicated form of domination in mind. He took some ice and towels and gave me a sort of rubdown. It felt wonderful.

Tell me about the El-Sinian mysteries, I said.

That stopped him for a moment, then he smiled. "Not too mysterious, are they?" he said. And then, feeling more force must be demonstrated, he scrabbled away the towels and tried again—but it just wasn't working. I felt myself smiling at his frustration, but forced the corners of my mouth down—must be careful now.

"It's too damn *frigid* in here," he sighed. "I can't stand it. Let's go home."

Where are you living now, Nils?

"I've got a nice place now. Not as nice as yours. I bet you've got a pool."

Yes, and a little Swedish sauna.

"That would feel so good . . . ."

AR

I just lay there pretending to be insensitive.

"Well," he said finally, "let's go out and at least warm up a little."

We checked out of the Inn and went bummelling down Main Street. Nils bought me an ice cream cone. We stopped in Art's Books, where they had a first edition of Madonna's *Sex* on display. Nils charmed the owner into letting him open the protective bag and show me his favorite pages.

One of the better boutiques had some panne velvet gowns in its window. Nils asked me which one I liked best. I said the cherry red one. We went in to see if they had my size. Nils came in the fitting room to help me try it on. He approved it, and insisted on putting it on his Gold Card.

I wore my new dress out on the street. It was nearly eleven by then, and Nils suggested we stop by the Mango Room to see what was happening there. It was Funky Night. The music sounded irresistible. "Oh, let's go in," said Nils.

Nils ordered us brandy alexanders, but I was too excited to drink. The last few years the Mango Room had become a student dive, but there was a great crowd there that night, nearly all grown-ups, of the refreshing variety of sexual persuasions that makes for the best dancing. Nils went to the deejay and asked her to play "Jungle Love." "You mean the Steve Miller or the Time one?" she asked.

"This *is Funky* Night," Nils said severely.

We danced to "Jungle Love" (the Time version), "Tina Cherry," "Knee Deep," "Alligator Woman," "Irresistible Bitch." It was then that Nils and I consummated our physical relationship in the only way possible now. You can't imagine how we danced. We closed out the Mango Room. "Time to go home now," said Nils determinedly, putting both arms around me as if frightened I'd try to run. "Where do you live?"

You must be afraid to take me home to your home, I said. You must have somebody else there.

"No, I swear, nobody's ever lived there but me. But you wouldn't like it there, it's all black and red with whips and snakes. It's like a stage set. You know, to impress people. I don't really like it. I bet I'd like your place though. Where are you going?"

I've got to get my car, I said.

"I'll drive you there."

It's just up the street.

"I'll follow you then," said Nils. "Don't want anything to happen to you."

I left him parked and waiting outside the entrance on Prescott Street, then, quickly as I could, with my lights out, pulled out of the University Street exit. He was nowhere in sight. Just in case, I took the extra long way home around Silvery Lake. By the time I got there, he was waiting for me.

I got out of my car, he got out of his. We stood in the doorway. Pang had probably been waiting for me all night. I could hear her scrambling around at the door, and then she started to cry. I have to go in, I said, and went in.

"You're not shutting me out," he said, against the other side of the screen.

I've got to go to bed now, I said.

"You're terrible to me," he said.

Now this shocked me. No I'm not, I said.

"Yes you are. You don't like anything I do, you never liked anything about me."

You know that isn't true.

He leaned against the screen, bulging it dangerously. "Then let me *in*," he said.

I shook my head.

"We have unfinished business," he purred.

Yes, I said.

"Why won't you let me in?"

Because I know you vampires, I said.

(He wasn't expecting *that*.)

I know the rules, I said. If I let you in, then you can come in any time you want. And I can't stop you. But you can't ever come in if I don't let you.

He gave a sick sort of smile. "Yes I can."

Try it, I said, and shut the door, locked the locks, put on the alarm, then went up to bed. I'd forgotten the salt, but it was too late for that anyway.

I heard Pang barking, and I opened my eyes, or, at least, I saw. I was lying on my back and the room was very dark, but I could make out the shape, the solid form. I couldn't move. I tried to shout but my voice box was paralyzed, and all I could force out was a sort of pant: haah, haah.

He came over. The bed bounced. I felt knees on my chest. Claustrophobic panic fear came over me. His breath wet my face. I tried to scream but just that panting sound came out.

Suddenly Pang's face thrust in, snarling. My head knocked against the wall; I thought my eardrums would break from the screams. I might have been knocked out for a minute. But then the weight on me was gone; I could breathe and move, and I opened my eyes to see Pang scampering out of the room. My face was wet and I could smell and feel it was blood, though I turned on the light to make sure.

I went looking for Pang, to see if she was all right. She was in the kitchen, licking her lips and wagging her tail. Her little jaws were soaked in blood.

Gently I felt around her little snout, then opened her mouth. She didn't seem to be in any pain, and I couldn't see any missing teeth or imbedded objects, or any sign of where she could be bleeding from. I got a wet towel and wiped her down, checking again for bleeding places. I couldn't see any wounds, and no fresh blood. Maybe she had just had a nosebleed. Did dogs have nosebleeds? I'd have to ask Padraic.

I gave Pang a bath. Again, there was no sign of a hurt on her. I took the sheets off the bed and put them in the washer, and tried to clean up what blood I could. There were spatters everywhere. All over the floor, the furniture, the wall—I looked at my little dog and wondered, how had she gotten it up *there*?

I took Pang to see Padraic first thing the next morning. He looked her over carefully, and said he did see a little flap of skin on the roof of her mouth, as though something hard and sharp had scraped across it. But that didn't look like it would have bled that much. Otherwise, she seemed fine. "Nosebleeds with dogs are not that common a problem," he told me. "If she ever does it again, will you call me? I'd be interested to see it happen."

Nils never told anyone what happened to his nose. Not even the doctors could figure it out, Laura told me. It was highly strange. When she'd seen him the first time after he came out of the ER, what struck her was that there wasn't any projection out from the bandages at all; in fact, they went concave a little where it went inward between his cheekbones. Of course that's what bandages would do, without anything to support them there.

Then about a month later she saw him in the hospital cafeteria. She knew it was him right away, she said, from the eyes and the hair, though he'd changed so much. He was wearing street clothes, an old gray T-shirt and dirty black jeans. He had the bandages off, and there wasn't anything else covering his face. "The room just cleared out in about twenty seconds," Laura said.

Even for her it wasn't easy to look at, but she said from what she saw he didn't seem to be healing very well. It made her queasy thinking about the potential for infection, there in the cafeteria. She guessed he was probably on some very strong drugs; his movements were very slow and vague. He had a pint of milk and a plate of Jell-O on his tray. After a few minutes he got up, without having eaten, and wandered across the room, around the corner where the coffee machines were and back towards the kitchen. She didn't see him come out again. They probably led him out the back way. And that was the last anybody saw of him.

He could come after me. After all, he's probably still alive. But he's not a fool, he knows a balance has been effected between us. Better to leave it that way than lose what he's got left. So mote it be.

That fall was just the best, for me and the coven. All the evil rottennesses seemed to have lifted. For Samhain I had a big costume party; everybody came and ate and danced all night. Dana and her husband brought their little girl Astarte, six months old, dressed as Baby New Year.

The best thing about that new year was my new job. It was about as far removed from SMAT as you can imagine, although the people were equally crazy; they were just more my kind of crazy. It was at the university. I would be Administrative Associate to the Department of Theater, Film, and Television. What the hell did it mean? Well, I would answer phones and sort their mail, do their internal newsletter and webpage, coordinate traffic in and out of the department head's office, and clean out the coffee machine every night.

This was the sort of plum you only got through connections. Well, I had them; I'd worked with several of the profs there over the years in community theater, and I was a former student of the head of their costume shop. Also, a covenmate of mine who worked in the video production unit had written a recommendation for me.

I started on the low end of the pay scale, but that scale had a very attractive rise to it. I could live very well on money like that. And the thing about university jobs was that once you were in, it was much easier to get hired for new openings than if you were an external candidate. As long as you did your best and behaved yourself, your career was more or less made. And there were benefits: health insurance and a retirement plan, day care if you had kids, a discount on tuition for university courses.

As it turned out, my summer housesit turned into a fall and winter one as well. One of the daughters of my friend who owned the house got seriously ill, and since they were in Canada she was getting fantastic treatment through their national health service. But they had to stay till she got better; my friend was only a part-time instructor at the university, so the little girl wasn't covered by their good health plan, and her husband's managed care insurer, which did cover her, refused to pay for her treatment back in the States. It would have cost them their house, their savings, everything, if they had brought her home. I could have done without this sad stroke of fortune, but Pang and I loved that house and did our best to keep it nice for our friends' eventual return. The only drawback to living there was it was a little too thrilling trying to get into town through the snow and ice on those back roads; the main road was still torn up and impassible, and the city council and planning commission were saying that because it was such a massive job it might not be ready till next spring. Poor Dave, no light show for him that year.

My plan was to live like a cockroach for the next few years until I had saved enough for a down payment on a house. There were some really pretty areas outside of town, like Maple Lake, where the militiamen weren't too thick and the property values hadn't been run up too outrageously by the upscale university types. I could quite reasonably afford a nice little place with a yard for Pang and my herb garden, and an extra room for my sewing machine, and a parlor with thick drapes where I could carry out my rites without interesting the neighbors.

Taking my place in the Department of Theatre, Film and Television, where everyone around me seemed grateful at how *normal* I was, was like fitting the last piece in the puzzle. I felt like a respectable citizen, ready to come out of hiding and live again.

I could hunt down another man, a sane one this time, even try to have a baby. Then again, I could . . . not. That was fine also; that didn't mean I had to be alone. I had Pang, after all. I might even get a companion for her so she could stay at home instead of having to go to Padraic's for day care. Maybe I'd find a beautiful little black-and-white shih tzu that would be like a puppy to her. I always thought that of the two of us, Pang would make the best mother.

Not long after I started working at the university, I was pawing through the remainders at Word Up—I was famished for new books, after my summer-long unemployment austerity measures—and saw my ex-husband had had a new book out. *Bound for Glory: The Art of Sexual Murder*. There, in full-color plates, were all those posters I'd paid for that had hung on my walls, that had given me nightmares, that I technically owned, because they were supposed to have been part of my divorce settlement. I almost bought it for old time's sake.

Sometimes I wish I had the stomach for true crimes. People like my former husband and Nils, who can not only face the cruelest aspects of this world head on but absorb them advantageously into their own characters, seem to have an easier time operating in life. But come to think of it, there's no reason to assume they have any advantage over me. I may not be strong and arrogant; I may never be. But I am brave. I know my craft. And I have friends.

My adventures have been quiet ones, compared to the case histories in my ex-husband's files. Still, it's been really, really weird. Sometimes it's all I can do to love my fellow humans, now that I've seen what they're capable of. And I've got to either love them or run screaming from them. Even so, I'm starting to think I have it in me to take a little of this world and tame it, gentle it into something I can live with peaceably. Maybe I can even teach it to dance, in a magic circle.

THE END